Love & Pomegranates

An Anthology of Short Fiction

Edited by
Rona Murray and Garry McKevitt

Sono Nis Press

VICTORIA • BRITISH COLUMBIA

CANADIAN CATALOGUING IN PUBLICATION DATA

Main entry under title:
Love and pomegranates

ISBN I-55039-I08-9

I. Canadian fiction (English)--20th century.* 2. Short stories, Canadian (English)* I. Murray, Rona, 1924- II. McKevitt, Gary.
PS832I.L68 2000   C813'.0108054   C00-9I0642-I
PR9I997.32.L68 2000

Sono Nis Press gratefully acknowledges the support of the Canada Council for the Arts and the Province of British Columbia, through the British Columbia Arts Council.

Electron micrograph photos reprinted by kind permission of Norman Wessells, Richard Linck, Diane Woodrum *Biology*, Random House, Toronto, ON. 1988
C.K. Pyne, *Atlas of Cell Biology*, Lippincott Williams & Wilkins, Philadelphia, PA

Photo credits for page 91: (top left to bottom right) Richard Linck and Diane Woodrum, Daniel Friend, C.K. Pyne, Norman Wessels.

Cover and interior design by Jim Brennan

Published by
Sono Nis Press
P.O. Box 5550, Stn. B.
Victoria, B.C. V8R 6S4
Tel: 250-598-7807
www.islandnet.com/sononis/

Printed and bound in Canada

Contents

INTRODUCTION 4

Norma DePledge
  A PHANTASMATIC PLACE OF CALM 13

Susan Trower
  HENRY R. BLOCK 23

Bill Stenson
  THE ONLY SIGN OF FIRE 31

Kristin Reed
  PERVERSIONS 43

D. H. Carley
  BENNY GOT A GUN 49

Alisa Gordaneer
  THE DOCK 59

Joe Abernethy
  THE TERMINAL CANOPY 69

Joanna Zilsel
  LIFE IS FRAGILE 85

Terence Young
  FAST 93

Cathleen With
  THE ARBUTUS TREE 107

kbanks
  ON LOVE AND POMEGRANATES 117

Kathryn LeCorre
  VIVALDI'S FOUR GYNECOLOGISTS 121

INTRODUCTION

As with its companion volume *Threshold*, a collection of poems, *Love and Pomegranates* concentrates on younger writers: some have barely graduated from university, others are beginning to be recognized. Most have published to a limited degree only, or not at all. The material is occasionally raunchy and explicitly sexual: "The Arbutus Tree" and "Perversions"; wildly humorous: "Vivaldi's Four Gynecologists"; ironic but not unsympathetic: "Henry R. Block"; dream-like, suspended in emotional shock: "A Phantasmatic Place of Calm"; surreal: "The Terminal Canopy"; or written with the shorthand of poetry: "On Love and Pomegranates." No matter what the approach, method, or subject matter, however, virtually all are concerned with loss and isolation although they were not chosen because of any uniformity in theme; they were selected because of the skill with which they are written. It was not until I looked at them as a group in order to write an introduction that I recognized a common thread binding them together, and also recognized, thankfully, that despite their clustering around a comparatively similar sense of alienation, not one of these stories is sentimental, self-pitying, or self-indulgent. The common theme, marked in some and slight in others, is no doubt simply part of the *Zeitgeist* at the end of the millennium.

If you look at the first paragraph of the first story, "A Phantasmatic Place of Calm," for instance, you find the writer has skilfully distanced herself from her subject (loss, betrayal) through a haunting image: "Calm takes over when you least expect it to, when you see your arm severed from your body in your own basement, for example, by the ripping blade of a table saw. . . . Your hand is vivid on the concrete floor, the palm upturned, the fingers slightly curled. Your life line and your heart line intersect and it dawns on you that you have never taken stock of that before and that it is enormously significant. . . ." From the phantasmatic place of calm the protagonist inhabits, exemplified by this detail, the story moves, almost casually, into the cause of the shock, her husband's remark: "Roseanna is moving in." Roseanna is her best friend. She is losing her husband and best friend at the same moment—a kind of double death. Norma DePledge gives the husband and wife no names, again enhancing the numb distancing. We know them chiefly through the details of their furnishings, the breathing "sheers" across their windows, the mementoes collected on journeys; we engage with Roseanna's warmth, energy, fun through small, lively incidents. The plot is mundane; the writing so masterly that the story remains embedded for a long time in the reader's consciousness.

Susan Trower also uses metaphor to explicate the meaning of her character's life; in this case, ironing. At one time, few activities were more boring or time-consuming than ironing. Today with our contemporary cottons and nylons, this domestic chore is outdated: not, however, for Trower's protagonist, also nameless, who on occasion even irons the living room carpet. Her life is so empty, she obviously has almost nothing to do, but the obvious is never stated. We know her everyday existence immediately, but she, and of course we see through her eyes, does not know it; she regards herself as competent, busy, reasonably attractive, and sensitive. We know her "gentleman caller" is embarrassed, longing to get away, aware of her unrequited and pathetic passion for him and with her on his annual visit only because he needs her business, but she believes he is falling in love with her. He forces himself to drink coffee and eat the rich food she has planned on making for months. The text gives us trivialities; the subtext indicates chasmic isolation.

Bill Stenson's "The Only Sign of Fire" and Terence Young's "Fast" have some similarities. The protagonists in both stories are young fathers whose married life, for one reason or another, is losing its charm. A usual plot. Nothing to it, except their idiosyncratic choices: they both become detached observers, not voyeurs exactly, by watching or trying to watch life unfold through windows. They isolate themselves, choose to leave the family warmth without leaving the family location. Stenson's protagonist has more reason to detach himself than Young's. He needs to escape, and his action is the more bizarre and the more humorous; Young's character is psychologically adolescent and proceeds to set up an exotic imagined reality to escape his tedious job and the conventional financial chains beginning to imprison him. Neither story comes to completion; the reader is free to extend the action into his or her own conclusion.

"Perversion" remains with the reader long after the ten minutes or so required to read it because it's so odd but at the same time so truthful, unabashed, out front. Kristin Reed draws parallels: "I used to tell myself stories like normal people masturbate. In secret, alone. Then I started writing stories and, when they were finished, I tore them up in tiny pieces, hid the scraps under banana peels and coffee grounds in the kitchen garbage. Like a pervert that exposes himself, but only when he is alone. . . . . A pervert who doesn't have the courage of his lack of convictions. Like a voyeur who peeks only into empty houses." Her protagonist (again without a name, a first person "I"), lonely after "another story," another broken relationship, briefly meets a "pervert": one who is equally lonely but has the courage of his convictions. Unwittingly, he helps her gain the same courage. There is no hurt in this story; there is joy. Ephemeral contact is achieved: "He turned and looked back so I bowed with as much arm-waving flourish as I could. . . . When I stood straight again, he was running directly into the sun. He leaped like a cartoon leprechaun, knocked his heels together once and kept running." A fiction writer, Reed suggests, is like that real pervert: telling stories joyfully, with conviction, not in secret to herself.

The other overtly sexual story, "The Arbutus Tree," is not joyful and does hurt. The tone setting the cast from society's underbelly is established at once: "There was a roller rink out by that condo fat-farm where old people hung out in their long grey undershirts. 'Come on, can we, please?' we begged every night there wasn't football on the transistor radio. 'No, you girls don't need to go up there and fool around like some cats in their hot heats,' Mr. Coopen said, a Marlboro hanging out of his mouth." The protagonist is adolescent, curious about and obsessed with the possibilities of sex; her friend Tanya is "no scaredycat." They are unwatched, untrammelled, essentially uncared for. Having seen two boys making mutual, messy love in a tree, they want that affection, but they learn their lessons the hard way since, for all their apparent toughness, street smarts, and bravado, they are unknowing. Cathleen With jumps with her narrative, leaves gaps, gives us virtually no exposition, characterizes through impressively tawdry dialogue, flourishes in the vivid contemporaneity of her style.

"Benny Got a Gun" by D. H. Carley comes out of the same cultural background as With's story; its superficially unattractive characters, without extended family or friends, have to look out for themselves with nothing more than a stretched, anxious bond between brother and sister. In the end that bond is presumably broken. The opening paragraph, again through its choice of language employed in interior monologue, sets up Lucy's life: "Every day it's the same old boring shit. Go to work each night in a stinking hot laundry, come home early in the morning, wander around the apartment, the sounds of the rest of the world buzzing in my ears until I can't keep my eyes open no more. Then I close the curtains, unplug the phone, put on my sleeping sunglasses, and hope some fuckstick with a mission from God don't decide to ring my bell and share the word."

When I came across these stories (and more), I may as well admit I was astonished and also intrigued. Had the young, well-groomed, smiling young women I saw in front of me lived the kind of life one presumably needs to have lived in order to write these kinds of stories? To capture this dialogue? How did D. H. Carley know what dropped out of sheets from hotels? What does a gun in the waist of your pants feel like? And what kind of life is it to have your only friend a revolver? "Not that this girl wants to pull a postie or nothing. My job may suck but I don't need to shoot up a bunch of people to prove my point. No, this is a private, personal thing, something between him and me. . . . I . . . don't say nothing about my new boyfriend." Lucy thinks of her little brother, Benny, and her description evokes his image instantly. We've known or at least seen people such as this who are uncomfortable in their minds or bodies, and we recognize what the symptoms imply: "That boy's hands never stop moving, swinging against his thighs or flapping through the air like a sparrow with a busted wing. He's always getting in shit. . . . He just sets himself up to be shot down. . . . Like that time soon after Momma died—a fast car, Daddy driving, a tree, don't ask. . . ." He's a loser. So is his sister. She sees herself with merciless objectivity as she poses before a mirror, practising with her "boy": "I do my Angie Dickinson, I'm a police chick and I look fine stance, legs spread apart, both hands clutched tight round the hardness of my boy, pointing him straight between my eyes. . . . Okay I wouldn't be mistaken for Angie in a dark alley by a blind man pissed out of his gourd, but I'm doing the best I can for a short skinny chick with bad skin and shoulder-length dirty blonde hair."

Two of these stories have what may be called a faintly ethnic origin. Their structure and tone are closer to the end of the twentieth than to the beginning of the twenty-first century in that they are not as edgy as those we have been discussing. "The Dock" by Alisa Gordaneer and "Life Is Fragile" by Joanna Zilsel are gentler: nostalgic and young in the best sense of the words. Gordaneer's opening is already in the past: "Hot as a bread oven, that summer hung behind our eyes. It stretched warm days into mosquito-plagued nights scented with tired grass, rotting fruit, and wilting roses, the thirsty garden a nagging character in our hot-pillowed dreams." This is a story of children in the garden, but is not in any way sentimental in a Victorian manner. This garden is filled with blackberry thorns and early wars between the sexes; with the saving values of the old who have survived want opposed to the careless indifference of the young who have not had to; with the prudence of the female, the stock root survivor, opposed to the churlish vanity of the male. The warm caring of the best in Finnish culture is as golden as the apple Kirsti holds in her hands at the end of the story.

Joanna Zilsel also writes in the first person in "Life Is Fragile" and once more the protagonist is young and female, an adolescent rather than a child. The reader has a sense that this fiction grows from the heart rather than from formal training in how to write. It is leisurely, without the detail that generally makes fiction solid. Its impact lies in the entrance it gives the reader into the feelings of a shy, vulnerable girl and her counterpart, a brilliant young man who, a molecular biologist unable to sustain himself emotionally in a bleak foreign culture, commits suicide. We enter David Chang's psyche only through Jen; through her own aloneness, we know his. The fiction is as delicate as the organelles, "the almost unfathomably miniscule inner components of cells" she, by chance, finds in David's textbook some time after her imaginary lover's death.

Ron, the protagonist in Joe Abernethy's "The Terminal Canopy," is travelling alone "up the coast." The actual area is never specified and the writer, although giving concrete, recognizable details, soon indicates the narrative is dream-like, Kafkaesque, and lived through a nauseous haze by a self-conscious and isolated narrator. Disappointed, this narrator tells an armless woman whom he meets while waiting for his final embarkation: "Very little happened . . . that was not ordinary." The woman insists he make "final arrangements" and after he has vomited from sunstroke, "he could feel her hand stroking his back and was briefly comforted by the sensation. He then realized that such a thing would be impossible. . . ." The woman knows far more than he does and has a secret agenda. The wounded bartender in a solitary establishment also appears to know him and is not surprised at anything that occurs; much later, he reappears under extraordinary conditions, saying, "You, sir, made very poor arrangements." Dreams contain symbols, are inconclusive; we are left to puzzle over the unknown narrator's "manner of travelling." What is conclusive is that nothing that happens after his meeting with the armless woman is ordinary; he receives far more than he has bargained for.

Abernethy's story is fairly long with odd incidents and details which appear unimportant but are not. kbanks' fiction, on the other hand, is condensed almost to the point of non-existence. Perhaps it's a prose poem. Told in the present by a nameless protagonist, it contains a single image which contracts the entire meaning of the fiction into itself: a pomegranate. The fruit, of course, has been used by other writers as a symbol of sex: its blood red juiciness spurts with life. The dead tabletop, simulated wood, at which the narrator stares in a state of suspended animation, acts as the base on which the fruit is first broken and then emptied into a husk after "she" has methodically eaten it, and he is finally able to move: "with [his] heart still lying on a paper towel" splattered with rubies of blood.

Kathryn LeCorre, writing in the first person in "Vivaldi's Four Gynecologists," treats bizarre loss with hilarity. She opens with a stunning declaration: "I lost several teeth and two ovaries this year, along with my uterus and mother." Then: "It has been a year of mourning one body part after another, first the parts and then my mother." She worries "about the Second Coming of Christ and if, when the dead are raised and we are given our incorruptible bodies, will they be exchanged part for part? And if so, will my assorted teeth and shrivelled ovaries rise from unexpected places . . . the shoreline of Japan . . . Vancouver Island?" She dreams in her displaced state after surgery and her fiction becomes recognizable as a Freudian travesty of repeated symbols involving beautiful women with perfect teeth, her gynecologist with his thin, expensive gold watch, and her uterus turned into a jaunty evening bag. She satirizes the medical profession with its well-degreed doctors floating in shoals of nurses, and she considers the ineptitude of her husband and four daughters who play with her hospital bed and eat her food on visits. When she returns home, her full-breasted daughters have taken her place in the usual sequence of things, dating replicas of her gynecologist. LeCorre is facing our universal fears—aging, a decaying body, being replaced and relegated to the back room—and she is doing it with consummate humour. In the final analysis, what else have we got?

"Vivaldi's Four Gynecologists" makes a fitting conclusion to this small book. It points a way to handle the losses, fears, nightmares which too often consume our lives. It concentrates, wastes no space, and it explores with humorous exactitude the psyche of the protagonist. She is unnamed, like so many characters in this collection. In my opinion, she becomes more universal than any of them with her lost teeth, ovaries, uterus, and mother, but with her jaunty self intact.

What makes a short story? Who knows? Poe laid down rules; many have laid down definitions. On examination, although some of the language used in these fictions is vernacular in the extreme, most of them fulfill the expectations of the short story: believable characterization, sufficient development, excellent dialogue, the twist of plot which keeps us reading. All are contemporary in that they dispense with introductory exposition, allow symbol or image to carry the full weight of explication, and manage to give the reader a clean, instant rendition of a moment in our history.

Rona Murray

NORMA DePLEDGE

Norma DePledge's fiction has appeared in the *Malahat Review, Room of One's Own, Grain,* and *Atlantis,* among other publications. In addition to writing fiction, she has—in collaboration with a colleague—recently completed a writing text-book for Prentice Hall Canada. Norma teaches English at the University of Victoria and at Camosun College.

A Phantasmatic Place of Calm

CALM
TAKES OVER
WHEN YOU LEAST EXPECT
IT TO, WHEN YOU SEE YOUR ARM SEVERED

FROM YOUR BODY IN YOUR OWN BASEMENT, FOR

example, by the ripping blade of a table saw. Suddenly the world is silent; you no longer hear the scream of machinery; you don't feel pain. You're mesmerized by things that, prior to that moment, didn't matter, weren't connected: the stitches on the neckline of your husband's vest, the knife-edge of a skate blade hanging from a hook beside the furnace. Time hasn't stopped, but it's been fiercely shoved aside by the seething details of indiscriminate reality, which are sharper and more insistent now than they have ever been before. Your hand is vivid on the concrete floor, the palm upturned, the fingers slightly curled. Your life line and your heart line intersect and it dawns on you that you have never taken stock of that before and that it is enormously significant; but then the sawdust in coagulating blood looks like toasted coconut and you know that when you were ten and your grandfather took you to the slaughterhouse three days after Christmas, you got blood in the tread of your running shoes and the patterns they made on your bedroom floor were tire patterns, not coconut, and suddenly you wonder if you should call your mother—because you think that today may be her birthday and you haven't made a cake.

You don't scream or run out of the room. You have no sense of urgency. You're buffered by an envelope of dead, hermetic air, yet beyond it, you can see electrons spinning. They say that when one of our senses is compromised, the others compensate. So it is with this. Sensation is now paralyzed, but your vision has gone manic. You cannot stop the flood of details coming in; neither can you feel them; nor can you send a single impulse out. They record themselves upon an empty screen. Your nervous system has shut down.

Shock is not a sudden, violent blow, an impact or collision, or a fierce encounter. It's the collapse of all the circuits between your knowing and your being. It's a state in which cause is severed from effect, impetus from action. It's the failure of all frames of reference, the place of no response, a phantasmatic place of calm.

My husband said, "I need to tell you something. I think you should sit down. Roseanna is moving in."

"Moving in?"

"We're in love."

"Roseanna?"

You have a vague sense that you should be surprised, but suddenly you've lost your ability to process information. Communication between your brain and your body has failed.

"Roseanna who?" you ask.

"How many Roseannas do you know?"

My Roseanna? Roseanna whom I laugh with in the rain, whom I turn to when things fall apart? That Roseanna? Roseanna, whom I love? The friend in whose arms I cry when I have no one else to trust? The one I told that I was crumbling? Her? You don't mean her, do you? You can't mean that Roseanna. There must be a mistake.

Those thoughts happen to you. They burst in through your skin, but you don't literally think them. You don't literally think anything, because something has clicked off. You heard it click, but you can't locate the sound. You have no memory of what it was, or what it would be like if it clicked on again, so you can't think of what to do about it. You can't even think for sure about whether or not something should be done. You feel as if you've been cored, like an apple, or eviscerated, though not in a painful way. Nothing hurts, but where your inside used to be is now a vacuum. It's what matter would be like if it were white noise. You hear your husband say, "Don't you think you better breathe?"

"It happened on the camping trip," he says. "We couldn't help ourselves. It's chemistry."

"Is it *my* Roseanna that you mean?"

Later there may come a time—years later, perhaps, when cause is once again connected to effect, when the wires are at last restrung between your being and your knowing—that you scream, or crumble in hysterics, or pummel your fists against an innocent chest in rage, but you don't do that until there's someone standing by that you can trust to hold the world together while you fall apart.

A man who lived in my hometown got his arm cut off in the machinery that sets the pins at a bowling alley. When he was in hospital, he picked up a banana in his left hand and, absentmindedly, transferred it to his right . . . to where his right hand should have been. The banana fell on the floor. He laughed until he couldn't breathe. They came in and sedated him. When he came to, he finally started to cry.

What can I tell you about Roseanna and me? I know you'd like her if you met her. She's that kind of person. It's hard to sum a person up. They're never really what you say they are. Even a photograph can be a kind of distortion.

Roseanna is about my size and shape, but she's really pretty. She has a beautiful smile. She's one year younger than I am to the day. Isn't that an odd coincidence? If I'd had a sister, I would have wanted it to be her.

We joined S.L.I.M.—years ago. It was cheaper than Weight Watchers and we didn't have so far to go. Roseanna tends to put weight on around her hips; I gain it round the middle. She's crazy about ice cream. She and her husband owned a Dairy Queen. She used to bring home Buster Bars and ice milk cakes. Black Forest was one of her favourites. You could count on finding a puddle of it on her counter if she was having a bad day.

Her husband, George, didn't like fat women, not that Roseanna's fat, but he didn't like anything that was round. George wasn't any prize in my opinion, but he thought of himself as a ladies' man. Some women must have liked him because he had a few affairs. When she was pregnant with Ruthie, Roseanna gained a lot of weight and George was nasty about it. She got pretty down for a while, and scared her marriage was in trouble. She tried to pretend it wasn't happening and just be more cheerful, and when that failed, she tried to be seductive but that didn't work either. The more worried she got, the more she ate until finally she said she knew she couldn't quit eating till she had the truth, so she asked him if he didn't love her. He retorted, "Would I have married you if I didn't love you?" Then he added, "I'll let you know if anything changes."

We only went to S.L.I.M. about two times. If you gained a pound, you had to hold a pig throughout the meeting. I wrote down everything I ate and added up all the calories in this little book they gave us. I really wanted to lose. Then at weigh-in, the weigh woman said I gained one pound, two ounces. "Looks like you get the piggy," she said.

"You must have read it wrong," I argued. "I can't have gained. I never ate anything all week but lettuce and Melba toast."

"I have been weighing for seven years, dear," she said. "I think I can read the scales. Let's face it, nobody likes it when they're caught out." She laughed in a superior way and handed me the pig.

"Fuck this," Roseanna said. She shoved the pig at the woman and added, "You can stuff your porker. We're outta here."

She grabbed me by the arm, hauled me out to the car, and drove straight to the nearest DQ. We had three Buster Bars each and laughed all the way home.

When I went back to get my belongings, the house was empty. The back door was unlocked. The curtains on the kitchen windows bulged as I entered the house, and sighed as I closed the door behind me. In the silent afternoon, the only sounds were the fretting of a fly against a window and the ticking of the clock. I walked across the kitchen, through the dining room, to the door of the library where the sun soaked through the heavy velvet draperies. There were no footprints on the library carpet.

Someone must have vacuumed that morning. I could feel them in the room removing all the traces, all the evidence. The carpet in the library marks so easily it's like a recording. I didn't have the courage to step inside.

The plaster dog that came from a curio shop in Butte, Montana, was still on the hearth. The ivory peach, brought from Africa half a century before, was broken. Its carved stem and leaf lay beside it on the shelf. A sailor doll with Empress of France written on the rim of its hat, bought from a tuck shop on a ship midway across the Atlantic, still straddled the hurricane lamp in the corner. The woman in the tuck shop—funny how some things stick with you. She had a mass of auburn hair piled up on her head. She sold Callard and Bowser sweets. I don't know why I remember that. Kids remember the strangest details. Anyway, there's the doll, sitting on top of the lamp. That hasn't changed.

There was a photograph of me that used to be on the mantel. It's gone, but I guess that's to be expected.

The sun streams in the window, catches the angles of the banister as I climb the stairs. The fern on the landing seems to be thriving now. I was never good with ferns. It used to mope and look anemic, but it's starting to fill out. Maybe it's just accepted that here is where it's going to be. It casts feathery shadows on the wall. It's dropped a few leaves, I see, but I think that's normal for ferns. I pick them up and tuck them in my pocket. I always liked the place to look neat. It does look neat. It's very well kept.

I didn't expect to be alone when I walked into the house, through the unlocked back door, across the kitchen where the fly fretted and the curtains bulged and sighed, past the green rubber frog with its dill pickle back and one ruptured leg, crouching where it always had on the back of the sink . . . through to the dining room . . . I stopped there to run my fingers along the backs of the chairs. I didn't mention that before. I stained the table and chairs myself and varnished them. People say it looks like a very old suite, but it's not. It was new unstained wood when we got it. It smelled like lumber and outdoors.

The strand of beads on the tiffany lamp above the table is still broken. I was going to fix that, but I just didn't get it done. . . .

I didn't expect to cross to the library and watch sunbeams dance on the unmarred carpet, or climb the stairs to the bedroom, alone.

Everything is exactly as I left it. Nothing has changed. Except the photograph, of course. But that's to be expected. And the fern. The fern is definitely doing better than it was when I was looking after it, but then I was never particularly good with ferns. Also there's this mask . . . outside the bedroom door. It's changed. It had a crack starting to form along the forehead. That can happen when you buy something from a place that's tropical and humid and try to keep it here, in the sere dryness of the prairie. I took it to a gallery that specializes in restoration and wooden sculpture. They said they'd try to fix it. It was the week before—the week before that week. So of course I didn't go back. And now there's a different mask. It's like the other one; in fact, it's so similar I wasn't sure at first. But it is different. I can see that now. Slightly lighter in tone, I think. And the ribbons. There were no ribbons on the other one. This one has ribbons of brushed copra that dangle from its hair. If you weren't intimately familiar with it, you wouldn't know that something had been replaced.

I walk into the bedroom. The French doors are open. The sheers breathe gently. The wallpaper—that strip in the corner where the room wasn't square, where I wrestled for half a morning trying to get the pattern to match, it's restful now, and cool, despite the warmth of a June afternoon. I sit on the edge of the bed and listen. Is that the clock I hear? Or the tick of a fly against the screen, or the soft sigh of the sheers breathing against the French doors.

We've lain here on afternoons like this, naked together, listening to the sound of June, the whisper of aspen leaves, the drift of time. This is our bedroom. This is the cool sweep of its sloped ceilings, the white expanse of quilt, the huge round bed, the lace of the hanging lamp. I made the lamp by hand. This is the pale blue carpet. These are the French doors. That is the unmarred prairie sky beyond. Those are the sheers that breathe in the afternoon. Nothing has changed, not the warble of a meadowlark in the field across the way, not the whir of grasshoppers, the dry smell of prairie dust, not the tick of the kitchen clock, not the cool of blue and white, not the heat of June, nothing. I am above us and I look down, at our skin, at our outline, at our touching like cupped hands . . . and I see that she is in my body.

I need a breath of fresh air. I find it hard to breathe inside sometimes. I don't think I mentioned that I hung every strip of paper in this house. And painted, inside and out. You can see where I dripped paint, out here on the balcony, just over there, under the eaves. It got on the shingles and I only made it worse when I tried to wipe it up. Oh well. You'd never notice it if it weren't pointed out. You couldn't look up at the house and see it from the road or anything like that.

Down at the end of the sidewalk—you probably can't see it from here—the date that everything was finished is imprinted in the concrete. July 1, I believe it was, or June. Or it could have been October. Who remembers now? The days got all mixed up and someone wrote the wrong thing in the wet cement. Someone. Some person. Such interesting, non-committal words. So much can be left out with so little subterfuge. The concrete dried and what is written there became the date. The real date yellowed over time and finally faded altogether. Now the new one is the date, and the matter's closed. That's what happens. A person writes something down, and it becomes the truth. You can't necessarily believe even what's written in stone.

The view is lovely from here. There's the picnic table down by the driveway. Under the big old poplar tree. We never used it. It waited there for some moment in the future when we would be ready for it, some summer afternoon, some June perhaps, when we had nowhere to be but home. When that June afternoon came, if it came, we would go down by the picnic table under the poplar where the sun shot through the leaves, stained-glass green, some June afternoon when the French doors were open and the sheers breathed gently, when the clock ticked in the kitchen and the carpets had all been vacuumed. On that day, we would sit on one of the benches, lean our backs against the edge of the table, our legs stretched out in front of us. We'd drink a glass of beer maybe, or a cup of tea. Or we might not drink anything at all. We might just sit side by side and look up through the leaves, up toward the house, to the French doors and the gently breathing sheers. We might do that without drinking or eating anything at all off the picnic table. But that wouldn't mean that the picnic table was a waste—even though we knew that we might never have a picnic off it, might never eat off it or drink—because we planned that we would use it in our own way when the time came some June afternoon, and that would be enough.

The bowling pin man in the hospital in my hometown, who cut off his arm and dropped the banana, said that what hurt him most in the end was not so much the loss of his hand, but all the things that he might have done with that hand in the future and that, now, he would never do.

Years later, what do we remember? A phantom pain? The sharpened details of a photographic print? The promise of the days that might have been but weren't? A concrete record printed in the sand?

A friend came with me that morning as I set out to get my belongings. Her name was Donna. She didn't know my husband or Roseanna. She said she'd hate the pair of them if she did. I said I didn't think she would, but she said, "Trust me."

I drove my car; Donna drove the rental van. She had to drop off a key to her roommate or go to the grocery store—some errand that couldn't be put off. I don't recall exactly what it was. I knew she'd be a little bit behind me but I was going to wait in the driveway for her to arrive. I was going to ask her to hold my hand as we walked into the house. I was going to not go in alone. I didn't intend to drive so fast. I didn't intend to be standing in the French doors—my breath stopped while the sheers breathed effortlessly behind me—when she pulled into the drive.

"Sorry I took so long," she called up to me as she got out of the van. "I made the wrong turn at Midland." She dashed up the walk to the back door, let herself in, crossed the kitchen, bounded up the stairs two at a time. "How long have you been here?" she asked as she came into the bedroom. I was standing at the doorsill, half in, half out.

"Hmm," she said, nodding as she looked around the room, "nice." Then she turned back to me, and smiled gently. "You can come inside now," she said, holding out her hand. "I'm here. It's safe."

Together, we considered where to begin. I started to go through some drawers. She opened the closet, surveyed the clothes hanging on the rail. "Is this your stuff?" she asked.

"Hers."

Donna turned to me, disbelieving, held out her arms, folded me to her and hugged me tighter than a lover. "Bitch," she mouthed over my shoulder. "You want me to trash it?"

"No," I said, but I smiled.

"You know all that ice cream that was in the freezer?" Donna asked, after we'd driven back to the city and unloaded my stuff; after we'd returned the rental van and Donna had picked up a six-pack from the cold beer store; after she'd told me to sit on the floor in the living room of my new apartment so I wouldn't fall off and to drink at least three beers while she made the nachos and before I considered thinking; after she told me to eat them whether I wanted them or not, damn it, because she made them and I needed some nourishment and junk food was better than no food and besides, nachos have cheese.

"Yes," I replied. "It's hers. She and her husband owned a Dairy Queen. I figure she got it in lieu of alimony. There's got to be a thousand bucks worth of ice cream in there."

"I unplugged it," Donna said.

She held me in her arms and we laughed until, at last, I cried.

SUSAN TROWER

"Henry R. Block" is Susan's debut publication, although her words have also received recognition in the Victoria School of Writing's Postcard Contest and the Okanagan University College Poetry Sweatshop.

Henry R. Block

SHE IRONS EVERYTHING.
LOTS OF PEOPLE DO,
IT'S JUST ONE OF THOSE THINGS THAT

IS SELDOM MENTIONED. THERE'S THE AUNT WHO irons socks. And the grandmother who not only ironed her flannel nighties nightly before slipping them over her head, but also smoked a pipe, but that's beside the point. Really, ironing isn't a big deal, not something people talk about behind her back, hands covering their mouths so she can't read their words, phone lines buzzing with the latest news. That just doesn't happen when it comes to ironing; even in a small town people have better things to talk about.

She, not the grandmother but the granddaughter, irons socks daily just like the aunt and irons her nightshirt nightly, just like the grandmother who smoked the pipe. And once a year when she is cleaning her house for a particularly special visitor she puts the long extension cord on the iron and flattens her living room rug; one of those red, almost burgundy rugs with black and gold, and tassels on either end.

"There—that's better," she says. She, on her hands and knees, the extension cord tangled around one foot. "For my Henry," she adds with a smile.

Henry is a very special guest. A guest deserving of such ironing. A guest who comes to her front door and always, always knocks with dignity, not like most who thoughtlessly ring the doorbell. They are the ones she doesn't bother getting up for; doesn't bother peeking through the curtains to see who it might be. When she hears the knock she knows exactly who it is. Henry. Her Henry. He stands tall in the doorway. His brown, almost black hair slicked back showing off his clean, smooth forehead.

"He will be wearing his suit," she says quickly, "well, sports jacket, really. You remember—the brown plaid one that his shoulders fill so nicely? And those crisp brown pants, hmm, he looks so handsome in brown. And those shoes, polished, and socks that match his pants so closely it looks as though he isn't even wearing socks; as though his pants extend neatly into his shoes." The cat sits perched on her lap looking into her eyes, as he always does when she talks. She doesn't pat the cat, and he doesn't purr. They don't have that sort of relationship.

Every year it's the same. She waits for Henry. Months before his arrival she begins preparations. Daily she diets, and irons, and vacuums, and plucks her eyebrows, and shops. She needs to find the perfect dress. Not too fancy with bows and sparkles, but something that looks everyday and yet looks somehow more than everyday. Definitely it's not the type of dress one would wear to clean the toilet, but very obviously not a dress to wear to a ball either. This year she has chosen a polyester dress, red and low cut. She buys a matching red bra, with lace, just in case they get that far.

She pushes her cat onto the floor so she can iron the cushions that decorate her couch, and she bleaches the screens on the front door, and irons the welcome mat.   And she waits.

While she waits she sorts and gathers all the papers he will need. She collects them and puts them into a small box. She always adds a few extras that she knows aren't necessary. She puts these in to keep him longer.

"Oh, you bought a new fridge?" She recalls his words from the year before last as she washes the front gate and the doorknob with a scrub brush and Lysol. The very same gate and doorknob that will be touched by Henry's hands. The very same hands that will find themselves touching the flesh of the red polyester dress. "Oh yes I did, nice of you to inquire," was how she answered. "It is a rather nice fridge; it was delivered by two young men." She told him about the young men because she wanted to be honest with him; didn't want him thinking he's the only man who ever steps into her life. He was jealous, she knows this, but also knows he must learn.

And on the day he is to arrive, she sits in a freshly ironed chair for hours without moving. There is no TV, no radio, no book in her hands. The living room is dark, except for the glow of candles that sit here and there, and a dim tiffany lamp beside the couch where he will sit. She sits close to the front door, in her new ironed dress, in her new "will not come off" lipstick which is red to match the dress. It won't come off on anything. She tested it again yesterday on the bedroom mirror.

"This year I will sit beside him on the couch," she tells the air. The cat is outside now; it isn't allowed in the house during such an important visit.

Then, he knocks.

The knock of a man who knows his business.

She doesn't get up immediately. Doesn't want to look too eager. She waits for his second knock. She loves the sound of Henry's knock. She carefully rises from her chair so as not to wrinkle her dress. She opens the door and there he stands. In his best jacket and shiniest shoes and there she stands in her red dress, lace bra, and lipstick. Her throat tightens. She must clear it before she speaks.

"Henry, so happy to see you," she says at last. He mumbles and nods; he is always shy their first moments together. His eyes meet her eyes—only briefly, but he will open up. "Come in, have a seat, I've been waiting for you."

He sits on her couch. He doesn't lean back and wrinkle the cushions. She smiles; he has noticed her freshly ironed cushions. She stands for a moment and then awkwardly sits on her chair. She must wait for the right moment to sit beside him, his leg next to hers. They are silent for a moment, just long enough for her to breathe in his air. And then they talk about important things; personal things she has saved up all year for only his ears. Her Henry.

"I've put a little something into bonds this year." She breathes the words to him so quietly that he has to lean forward—towards her. She leans towards him. When he looks down she knows he can see her freshly ironed bra. When he looks up their lips are so close, if she could lean forward slightly they would touch, but she can't.

"I see," he says. His warm breath caresses her lips.

She doesn't bring him the box immediately.

She brings him coffee with cream. Then she feeds him. Men love to be fed, that's what her mother always told her. She's been baking. She brings him Chocolate Cream-Cheese Brownies and Lemon Squares and Pears in Chocolate Sauce. But soon, too soon, he has had enough. Enough talk. Enough food. Enough coffee. She knows this by the way he taps his pencil on the coffee table and looks towards the ceiling, but she waits. If she waits long enough he will have to ask her for it. She likes it when he asks. It gives him power. He doesn't handle power well and so she does this little thing for him as lovers do, to help him. It makes him uncomfortable.

"I will need your papers then," he says. At first he says it quietly. She pretends not to hear and begins to tell him about the neighbour's cat. She laughs a deep throaty laugh when she speaks of the moments of pleasure they, the cats, had under her window last night. She imagines she irons his pants, the iron gliding over the brown cloth creating a perfect crease; she runs her fingers down the crease.

"Your papers. I will need them." This time he says it louder. Not shouting but firmer, like his knock on the door. His nostrils flare slightly, not in an unsightly way, but just enough so she knows.

"Fine then," she says. Although she has been expecting it, she is still annoyed. This is how they fight. But she gives in easily, mostly because she has plans. When she returns she sits directly beside him. Their legs only inches apart. She leans over when she puts the box on the coffee table in front of him and her elbow touches his knee. Even through the material of her red polyester dress she can feel the crease in his pants, not as crisp as she would have it, but crisp like a single man would have it. She hesitates but only for a moment. This makes a small smile appear on his face, just enough of a smile that she can see a glimpse of his teeth. She didn't see his teeth last year.

He pores over each piece of paper, his eyebrows furrowed. Next year she will reach over and her soft hand will smooth his wrinkled forehead. She can feel his soft skin. He gently holds a pencil in one hand; his lips pucker ever so slightly as he looks through the box, almost as though they are preparing, thinking about kissing her own lips.

Then it happens. His hand reaches towards hers, exactly as it was meant to be; as if he is drawn towards her heat; as if destiny has brought them together. When his hand touches hers, his breath stops—she knows he is as relieved as she is; they have finally reached a turning point in their relationship. Now they can go on. His hand is smooth; he uses cream. He looks into her eyes; his eyes are big as lovers' eyes get at a moment of truth. She smiles at him. He doesn't smile back. It isn't a time of joy; it's a moment of ecstasy. Next time she will know how to act. He leaves his hand touching hers for a brief moment. Then, knowing the type of woman she is, he pulls his hand out of the box of receipts.

"My apologies." His eyes don't meet hers when he says it. She leaves her hand in the box, waiting for him to reach in again. But he is shy. He fumbles with the one receipt, putting it onto the table, then picking it up again and looking at it more closely.

"You had your cat fixed?" he asks as he examines the receipt, a vet bill.

"Oh yes, I most certainly did. It wasn't *my* cat under my window; you must have misunderstood. It was the neighbour's cat. Mine's not like that. Not anymore." She giggles and gives him a tiny slap on the knee. He doesn't move his knee away. He keeps it there—she knows he enjoys her touch. Knows he loves her, just as she loves him.

But then, all too abruptly, he gathers his things together and makes some poor excuse about having to get back to the office.

"Are you sure?" She talks quickly. "There's nothing else you need to know about me? Nothing we need to talk about? We've hardly talked. Are you sure you have everything you need? There's probably more. There's probably much more that should be discussed." She has been too pushy, too forward. She shouldn't have put the receipt about the cat in the box. It was a mistake. It has embarrassed him. He is such a proper man.

"No, really, I believe we are fine." He has reassured her.

"But you must need more than I've given you?"

"I'll phone you, I promise." He smiles but his eyes don't meet hers.

He puts on his coat and picks up his briefcase in one hand and her box in the other, leaving no arm free for an embrace. And he leaves. Leaves her standing at the door. She waits until he gets into his car and she waves. He doesn't see her kiss her hand before the wave, or does he? He waves back and smiles. The kind of smile that tells her everything she needs to know about love, and passion, and the way his heart beats when it comes in close contact with hers. She smiles back so that he too will know—everything. Before closing the front door, she calls the cat in. She returns to the couch, where she stands silent for a moment.

"He will call," she says. "He promised."

Then she sits exactly where her Henry sat (the seat still warm from his heat). "If only we hadn't fought so, maybe he would have stayed longer." She wipes a tear from her cheek. "Next year, we will not fight. We will not fight."

She picks up his mug and turns it in her hand, wondering where exactly he placed his thumb. Wondering where his fingerprints remain. She brings the mug up to her nose. She can smell his coffee; smell his lips; smell his breath captured in the mug. She brings the mug to her lips.

Her tongue finds the edge of the mug, where his lip prints remain.

Susan Trower

BILL STENSON

Bill Stenson is 5' 8" and teaches English at Claremont Secondary in Victoria, British Columbia. He is a co-editor of the *Claremont Review.* In this picture, Bill is in the background.

The Only Sign of Fire

LIFE
LOOKS A LOT
DIFFERENT FROM UP IN

A TREE. YOU SEE THINGS YOU DON'T NORMALLY SEE. OF COURSE I DIDN'T KNOW THAT when I climbed up into the tree. There are a lot of things about climbing up in a tree you don't know before you actually climb up. It's funny how life works that way.

Anyway, it was a Friday night I took the notion to climb up in the tree. It was my "night out with the boys," as Peggy liked to put it. Some nights I just don't feel like being with the boys and it's kind of informal down at the local pool hall—whoever shows up, plays. My game has been off lately and the cue hasn't felt at home in my hands.

It's actually quite a comfortable tree—a huge maple like the others that line one side of our street. When I say the tree was comfortable, it's not in a comparative way. I don't do this sort of thing as a rule, but the one in front of our house has a particularly large sloping branch that I find quite cozy. Instead of walking all the way into town, I stopped at the 7-11, bought a special thermal cup I'd always wanted, a ham and cheese sandwich, and headed back toward our house. The truth is I was planning on puttering around in the garage for the night, maybe stack the cord of wood I'd split. The blade on my band saw was dull and it's one of those things you never get around to.

So the next thing I know I'm sitting up in the tree that is right in front of our house with quite a nice snack and a warm cup of coffee in my new 7-11 mug. I'm thinking it would have been a good idea to have grabbed a Danish or a Sweet Marie, but realistically you can never come completely prepared to wherever it is you go.

It's amazing to me how life never seems to go like you've planned it. That's the way it is with me, anyway. If I had my life to live over I wouldn't plan a thing. Just go with the flow like a kite in the wind. A kite never knows when it will be dragged out of the attic and set free and I'm sure it doesn't care. A kite never plans anything. I certainly never made plans to climb up in a tree on a Friday night and I think that would have been okay if I hadn't planned so many things in the past.

The view was great from where I was sitting. I could see all the way to the end of the street and it felt like I could look right in on my own house. Peggy was moving around a lot. First one light would go on, then another room would light up. She finally settled down to talking on the phone. She's always on the phone and she's mastered the art of switching from ear to ear. Me, I get sore just ordering pizza. Talking on the phone doesn't so much apply to Peggy, now that I think of it: she mostly listens and uh-huhs. My wife has a lot of friends.

I thought maybe she'd be watching a movie. She's seen *Gone with the Wind* hundreds of times. I told her she should keep track on the calendar and send it in to the Guinness people. She told me it was the stupidest idea she'd ever heard and this made me think that some of the other ideas I'd come up with over the last seventeen years weren't so bad.

It was comfy with my hunting vest and my hot coffee. It was hot, too. I'd recommend one of those 7-11 cups to anyone in my situation. It really did the trick.

She was on the phone for a long time so I knew she wasn't talking to Jessie. Jessie's our fifteen-year-old who has a car-driving boyfriend. That's what they do a lot—drive around. Up and down our main street, mufflers rumbling, holding up two fingers to their friends who drive down the main street going the other way, like the peace everyone wanted while the Vietnam War was on was finally here, Jessie snuggled right up beside him, holding on for dear life, which can be hard to take for some dads. I figure Jessie has a head on her shoulders that knows what to do with the rest of her body. Peggy doesn't see it that way which is why I knew it wasn't Jessie on the other end of the line. Their conversations lately have been short and brittle.

Then the bathroom light went on, which didn't exclude her from still being on the screamer. We got a real deal on the cell, evenings and weekends. I can see why women like a fancy bathroom. I really can. Presentation means a lot.

I could swear there's a special kind of mayonnaise they throw on the ham and cheese. It's the kids working in there late at night that make them—I've seen them do it. Some genius deserves a pat on the back, I can tell you. It's either the mayonnaise or a secret spice.

From where I was sitting I could hear the pathetic bark of the McGintys' dog across the street. I feel kind of sorry for the mangy mutt, now that he's seventeen and nearly blind with cataracts. Poor thing wouldn't walk out of the yard if you left the gate open. It wasn't always so. Jason was afraid to deliver the newspaper after the dog took a bite out of his ankle. I don't get mad very often, but when your kid loses flesh it's time to stand up. That's why I know how old the McGintys' dog is, because he and Jason have been the same age since the McGintys moved in.

The vanity in the master bedroom is where the final touches are applied. The last layer, so to speak. When Peggy approached the three-panel mirror without a phone in her hand, it was clear that arrangements had been made.

When the garage door finally opened, Peggy started up the '56 Caddy. It doesn't sound like much but it's been completely redone, inside and out. They call it a vintage car, a genuine antique. I've got a couple of guys in town who've offered me an embarrassing amount of money for it but I couldn't sell the old beast. Some things in life become part of you after a while. Tony, who works down at a small independent on the edge of town, says if I use this special additive in the gas, the car will outlast me. I know Tony would love to buy my car—he's done most of the work on it over the years. I can't stop by for a tank of gas without him seeing me off by taking a rag out of his back pocket to massage the fenders. Tony never asks if I want to sell. Some people know better.

She wasn't heading over to visit her sister, that much was clear. Beulah only sees Peggy drive up in the old Toyota pickup that's wedged in beside my workbench. It's got a bit of rust and the clutch is slipping but it runs. The Japanese make it hard to sell. Grey, overcast skies sum up how Beulah sees the world. If you want to catch Peggy's sister in a good mood, wait until it's rained for three days in a row and invite her over to watch news coverage of flood victims in China. Put cream in her coffee that's off two or three days. There's nothing in the world Beulah has come across that doesn't need improving. She's been legally separated from her husband, Fred, for five years now with no sign of divorce. When she and Peggy get together it's time to review life's misery. Having to drive our old pickup truck can only stand in the shadow of Beulah's having put up with Fred, but at least it's something.

Driving away in the Caddy meant she was in the mood to taunt the brighter side of life. She drove right underneath me on the way out and stopped for a last-minute inspection in the rear-view mirror before heading into town. The left back-up light was out. It had to be new or Tony would have noticed it.

I didn't have to wait long. Finished the second half of my ham and cheese and she was back again. I wish she'd learn to take the curb gently and it's not that I haven't asked. The front shocks are on the edge and they're expensive. I can see she's not alone. Naturally, any man slouched in a maple tree outside his yard who sees his wife drive up with a man in the car would be curious and that was me to a T. I could tell right off it was Fred she had with her. Fred always walks with a cane and limps wherever he goes. I've seen him cross the kitchen floor, when he was still with his wife, and help himself to a beer with no cane and no limp. He said his father brought the cane back from the Boer War but I don't know how much of that to believe.

My first thought was Peggy had a plan. She was good at leading other people's lives. Maybe she'd had enough of her sister's stories of missing Fred one minute and despising him the next. Any minute Beulah would pull up for a game of crib that would turn out to be three-handed. These things are always touchy and after the weather you can always talk about fifteen-twos. The kitchen was out of the question from where I was sitting. Fred liked his beer and I was sure there were two or three in the fridge. Otherwise, he'd take Scotch straight up.

Fred eventually limped into the living room and Peggy followed. He took a seat in my leather wingback recliner I got second-hand after a house fire. Peggy put on some music. Music is always nice. It kind of soothes the nerves, makes you relax even if you're not in the mood. That's how I met Peggy in an off way. Everyone is angry at least one night in their life and I was bar-hopping after I'd been fired as a car salesman. Let go, Harry Stoke the manager said. Looking back, it was as it should have been. I hadn't sold a car in two months and cars were selling. I'd gone out, drinking up the nerve to slug someone in the face and I distinctly remember thinking that was what I needed to do to find peace. It didn't have to be Harry Stoke, anyone would have done. I ended up having a drink with Peggy Malone who wore a white pearl necklace around her neck. It was a fine neck and I could see why she wore a necklace there. We ended up back at her place and she put on some music. Albums in those days. I'd never heard such music before and I couldn't tell you the name of it to this day, but there I was, as comfortable as one could get on a smelly old couch with a dozen cats crawling up your leg, but relaxed. Music can do wonders.

The leaves weren't full out on the maple, but just the same I had to stand up to get a good view of the guest bedroom. Peggy got there first and I imagined Fred making a big production of hobbling up those stairs. He never went anywhere without his ancient pocket watch and long gold chain. I could envision the chain swaying side to side as he tilted his way up the stairs. I'm not even sure the watch worked. Any time you asked Fred what time it was, he always took a guess.

A dark night brings with it a fragile security. It can make the best of us unreasonably brave and a dark night on the second floor never asks for curtains. It didn't take them long to finish. Fred always struck me as an efficient man and to be fair, he may have felt time was against him. He used to peel an orange the same way.

It was the perfect venue for Beulah but she was nowhere to be found. Timing is everything. After Peggy drove off to return Fred to the bachelor apartment he'd taken, I decided to go for a walk. I was dangerously low on coffee and for some reason I felt the need for dessert. Sometimes the selection of sweets is so low, choosing is easy. There was a new clerk on and he was kind enough to point out which row of chocolate eclairs was fresh. I guess it didn't make any difference to him. I felt like telling him not to worry: the pimples that had blossomed around his nose would disappear in time. I thought better of it and wished him a good night.

It would have been more comfortable with a pillow but I did manage to catch some sleep up in the maple. Before I did, Jessie pulled up and her boyfriend had his stereo turned way down, which was nice. He walked her to the porch and all of the lights were out except for one in the kitchen. The two of them sat for a while, snuggling on the porch steps, sharing a discman. It was obvious they hadn't mastered the art of fondling but they were both open to exploration. Everything comes in stages.

Time flies by faster when you're up in a tree. I don't claim to have any scientific evidence for this, but I believe it just the same. Jessie came out on Sunday afternoon to look around the yard. It's not often a fifteen-year-old will take the time to look around the yard. I liked to think she was looking for me. Monday rolled around and the kids were off to school. Jason was late as usual. He's not a morning person and he takes showers that stop when the hot water runs out. Peggy left shortly after for work. She works down at the local health clinic where she counsels people on birth control and such. I hopped down and went in for a shower and a change of clothes. I'd decided to pop into the office and tell them I'd be out of town for the rest of the week. Most of my accounts were closed so it wouldn't be a problem.

It didn't take me long to make the tree more comfortable. I had some old wood around that was supposed to be made into shelves in the rec room. I made it over into two levels. There's nothing worse than living somewhere thinking there's nowhere else to go. I found the old down sleeping bag I used to use when I was into duck hunting, a few pillows. I ran a hose down the fence line and had running water available not more than ten feet away. Fresh air has a taste all its own in the unfolding leaves of a maple tree. It's the kind of thing I'd recommend to anyone.

By Wednesday, Peggy had got into the habit of meeting Fred for lunch at the house. If she skips her coffee break, she can take an extended lunch. The neighbours knew I was up in the maple tree, but Peggy didn't. Information can have big gaps when you least expect it. One day, old Mr. McGinty shuffled over when I was fashioning a make-shift closet.

"What are you up to, Hester?" he said. I've told him on more than one occasion that my name is Lester, but it's the kind of thing you let go.

"Building a tree house," I said.

"I thought so. I said to Eleanor last night when we were eating supper that it looks like Hester is building a tree house. You should have done it years ago when the kids were little."

He watched me for a while, steadied the ladder once or twice to make himself feel like he was a part of it all. His dog made a feeble attempt at lifting his leg to pee against the trunk of the tree. I don't know if it was a good thing or not.

Late one Saturday afternoon, Jessie came out and sat at the base of the tree and started painting her toenails. She loves gummy bears, particularly the black ones, so I dropped one down that I swear made a hollow sound when it hit her head.

"How's my little muffin?" I said.

"Dad. It's you. Where have you been?"

"You know me. Never far from home."

"We've been worried about you. Mom's beside herself."

It was hard for me not to tell her that this was not the case twenty-four hours a day. My reserve startled me. I explained as metaphorically as I could that I needed some time to myself for a while. It's not always easy to determine how much a fifteen-year-old can comprehend. I threw her down a few more black gummy bears and soon her boyfriend's muffler could be heard coming down our street. She asked if she could come and visit and I told her that would defeat the purpose of my being alone.

I had to straighten up a few affairs at the office and I had a few phone calls to make to out-of-town customers. I worked late into the night, I guess, because when I woke up slumped over my desk, the birds were starting to sing even though it wasn't yet light out. I helped Charlie at the 7-11 haul in the newspapers that had just arrived. He said I must be pretty anxious to find out what's going on in the world to be up at such an hour. He's a well-meaning kid, really.

When I got back to my maple tree, I was in for a shock. The electric cord I use for my weed whacker was strung from the house and up the tree and connected to the TV set from Jason's room. It's only fourteen-inch, but still. It's times like that when you realize why you bothered to have kids.

Kids will teach you stuff about yourself you don't want to know. Peggy didn't want any children at first. May have been the line of work she was preparing for. Life can be complicated enough without kids, she used to say, which implied that life would be too complex with them.

It didn't take long for Fred to move in. I could see it coming, I really could. I figured it had been at least a week since Peggy realized I was living in the maple tree right outside her front door, so what she was trying to pull, having Fred park his Impala down at the end of the street in the middle of the night and pack two large suitcases up the street and into the house, was beyond me. I was growing quite fond of my maple tree by that time, but a man living in a tree only sleeps in fits and starts. Some people don't need to practise being naive.

With rabbit ears I was able to pull in one station only, but it was better than nothing. The thing I liked about it was the loyalty you develop. The talk show host becomes your minister. Newscasters read you a bedtime story every night. I'd never given daytime TV a thought before but I can see now how people get hooked. It's easy to become immersed in the lives of people you know, and before you realize it you care what happens to them. Imagine having a twin brother dying of cancer and you've never lost a game of chess to him before and you know you should lose for his sake but you're afraid he'll know you're doing it out of pity which is worse than winning and so you feel trapped. Every day you play him in the hospice recreational room and every day you try to find a way to lose but as close as you get you keep winning and the net result is you feel like a loser. God, life is so unfair. This was where I was one day, watching a man tell his twin brother that he felt terrible being such a good chess player, bawling his eyes out, when I was interrupted.

"Lester, get the hell out of that tree. Right now. It's no place for a grown man."

Beulah had her hands on her hips which was the first stage of a tantrum. I wasn't so much surprised by her appearance as disappointed. I thought she'd have shown up weeks ago.

"Can't you see I'm busy, Beulah? You've picked a bad time," I said.

"How can you make such a spectacle of yourself? Here you are sitting up in a tree while your wife is shacked up in your own house with my husband. Don't you feel any shame?"

She did her little stutter step then, back and forth beside the tree. Whenever she got herself worked up, she found it necessary to fidget with her feet.

"I have nothing to be ashamed about, Beulah. This is my tree house and I built it all by myself and I happen to like it. I'm catching one of my favourite shows, if you didn't notice, and I'd rather not be disturbed."

"You're frittering your time away watching *Days of Our Lives*. For your information, you're watching a rerun."

"You're kidding."

"No, I'm not kidding. Sammy finally lets him win a game and his cancer goes into remission. Now I want you out of that tree this instant and I want you to throw my husband out of your house."

"Can't do it, Beulah. It's not my place to do such a thing. His cancer just disappears? I've heard of that happening before."

Beulah took off her shoes then, and started throwing them up at me. She has pudgy little feet with the middle toe longer than her big toe, just like Peggy. "Well if it's not your place, whose is it? You haven't turned religious or something, have you, Lester?"

"Would you like a hot cup of coffee?" I asked. "I don't have much room up here for visitors, but I could send a cup down if you don't mind it black."

She walked barefoot to the house and tried the garage door first. Of course all the doors were locked so she picked up one of the folding chairs from the porch and smashed the living room window. Had I been able to predict what she was going to do with that chair I would have told her we kept an emergency key under the garden gnome. The sound of broken glass tends to draw neighbours out of their houses. Just curiosity, I suppose. Some of the neighbours who weren't privileged with a satisfactory view began to gather at the sidewalk. There was definitely a ruckus going on inside and as Beulah made her way from room to room we were all able to follow her progress by listening to the sounds of smashing china, mirrors, the toppling of bookcases. By the time she made her way upstairs there was smoke making a straight line out of the chimney. She didn't break any upstairs windows, but instead opened them up and threw out a wide variety of clothing that belonged to Peggy and Fred. I hadn't realized until that moment that Fred favoured boxer shorts.

Bill Stenson

The only sign of fire was smoke coming out of the chimney but someone called the fire department anyway. They pulled up with sirens blaring and ran the hose from the McGintys' side of the street and smashed the front door down. What they found when they got in there I don't know but Rachmaninov was pouring out of the house. We always kept a fair selection of liqueurs on hand and Beulah may have been going through them by this time. While it's one thing I'll never know for certain, my guess is she never found one that suited her.

Things settled down soon after they discovered there was no real fire. Beulah came out, finally, and walked shoeless down the street, leaving her car as her signature. I knew it was just a matter of time before someone came home. Reruns aren't so bad if you've never seen them in the first place. The beauty of living in a tree is you never know what will happen next. Sometimes, I kind of like that.

KRISTIN REED

While raising her two children, Kristin Reed has written two novels and a number of short stories, one published in *NeWest Review*. She has worked as a cook, editor, seamstress, advocate, activist, and foster parent. Originally from Saskatchewan, she is currently living and writing full-time in New Mexico.

Perversions

SOMETIMES,
WHEN THINGS GET
TOO COMPLICATED, WHEN
STORIES COLLIDE, I LIE DOWN UNDER

A BLANKET ON THE COUCH AND READ A MURDER mystery. I put the Cowboy Junkies' tape on eternal play and read and then sleep until the stories are sorted. I use that tape because I like every bit of it, even the twenty minutes of silence at the end. An old lover recorded the tape for me as part of the loving/hating bewilderment of our separation.

If that was in a story, it could be that the ex-lover left the silence, didn't finish the tape, because he knew it would irritate. But that would be a story. In reality, the poor guy just couldn't finish anything. Not anything. Marriages, affairs, raising kids, fixing a roof. Nothing.

In a book, a murder mystery, I read that what writers do to put themselves to sleep is tell themselves stories. I was intrigued because that is what I stopped doing when I started writing. I didn't want to waste stories that belonged on paper by telling them to myself.

I had always felt guilty about telling myself stories, at night or any time. What if someone found out? What if someone caught me just having fun with myself? It would be like getting caught masturbating. Everyone does it but no one wants to be observed, caught at it. Except a few perverts, of course.

I used to tell myself stories like normal people masturbate. In secret, alone. Then I started writing stories and, when they were finished, I tore them up in tiny pieces, hid the scraps under banana peels and coffee grounds in the kitchen garbage. Like a pervert that exposes himself, but only when he is alone. In his car, or in the forest with no one else around. A pervert who doesn't have the courage of his lack of convictions. Like a voyeur who peeks only into empty houses.

I watched a man masturbate once, a pervert. He asked me to. I was standing right in the centre of a pedestrian overpass at about four in the morning, mid-summer, just starting to get light. Why I was there is another story altogether. The walkway was over an empty city street, quiet, near the university in a prairie city. The pervert, looking like a normal young man, approached the overpass at one side of the road so I turned to walk to the other side. He stopped, looked up at me, and put his hands into his pockets. He said, "Don't go. I just need to talk to someone," and walked closer to the ramp.

Because of that other story, the one about why I was there, I was in no mood for words so I didn't answer, just moved away at the same speed he moved forward.

"I won't hurt you," he said. "I'm just so lonely." The pervert stopped at the bottom of the pedestrian ramp so I stopped too, suspended over the far side of the road. He asked from across four empty lanes, "Do you live around here?"

Part of that other story was that I was so lonely, too.

Before we go on, you should understand that I don't consider "pervert" to be an insult. It means turned away from that which is considered right or normal. I realize that some of you may think that "pervert" is, by definition, a pejorative. But "normal" means average, usual, ordinary, regular, common, typical. One would think that "normal" could just as easily be considered a pejorative. Just think about being told that you're an "average" lover, a "typical" man or woman, or that your humour is just "ordinary." What if you are accused of giving the "usual" response, or told that your speech is "common"?

See what I mean?

So back to the pervert and me. We performed a sort of dance. He stepped back from the bottom of the ramp and I stepped forward at the top. He came closer, I retreated. The sky was light and I could see that he was very young, early twenties. All the time we danced, he asked questions, made comments, about the most ordinary things. With a tip of his head to the university buildings, "You a student?" and I nodded briefly. "You married?" I shrugged, unsure—that other story, remember. "What's your name?" I looked up to the pale sky. Maybe he didn't even realize, at first, that this was an unusual conversation about a so-common longing. But perhaps he did because his next question, in the face of my perverse silence, was, "Will you watch me jerk off?"

I didn't answer and I didn't leave. Was I the voyeur, peeking into what I hoped was an empty house?

He backed off a few steps, looked up and down the still-deserted lanes and opened his belt. The clinking of the buckle sounded with the early-morning bird songs. The sun was up just enough to cast his shadow so far behind him that it was lost in the hummocky roadside grass. His zipper sounded like . . . like a zipper being pulled down but so loud that I looked around to see if that very ordinary noise had alerted anyone to this unusual roadside activity. No one but the birds and us.

Above him, I walked closer, right to the end of the overpass, where it bent and fell away in a shallow ramp. I looked down at his dark, wavy hair. He looked up and when I slid my hands into my jeans pockets and leaned my hips against the railing facing him, he dropped to the ground, fell on his back, raised his hips and pulled his pants down past his knees. There was quite an erection rising straight up from the patch of dark hair that extended, thinning, down his legs and up under his shirt. He had on a pale green T-shirt and an open denim jacket. Just an ordinary young man in normal clothes. An average dresser.

He must have been in pretty good shape because, while he used both hands to manipulate his penis and testicles, his hips remained off the ground. He kind of rested on his feet and shoulders, his body a straight line from knees to neck, an isosceles triangle if you include the line from his nape to his heels. The third side of the triangle was formed by his slanted shins, covered with wrinkled-down dark grey corduroy. He didn't make a sound, but I was fifteen feet or so above him so maybe he did keep up the flow of quiet words that is the usual with some people during sex. I thought it was normal, in that circumstance, not to be looking at his face.

I watched until the sun caught the rise of semen above his hands and then, as he collapsed, triangle to line, I looked around at the morning. The sun was definitely up and very warm. It would be another in a series of long, hot prairie days. The air still smelled damp and fresh, though. When an engine of some kind started up behind one of the university buildings, the pervert squirmed around and pulled up his pants, reversing the zip and buckle that made entirely different sounds closing than they had opening.

He stayed sitting, knees drawn up, head down, so I walked down the pedestrian ramp and onto the grass. His jacket was dark across the shoulder with dew and there were bits of dry grass caught in the wavy hair on the back of his head. A car went by on the farthest lane, then another close beside us. He stood up and after a moment looked at me. I let him look.

"Thanks." He stuck out a hand, then pulled it back and wiped it, palm and back, on the corduroy over his hip, stuck it out again, still looking. I took his hand, nodded, looked away, around at the trees and buildings and shadows, before I let go.

He turned away and walked along the roadside. I watched him go, wishing that this was a story I was telling to myself because then it could end differently for him and for me. Or then it could just end. He turned and looked back so I bowed with as much arm-waving flourish as I could, copying Errol Flynn sweeping off his much-plumed foppish hat, circling it down and across the grass. When I stood straight again, he was running directly into the sun. He leaped like a cartoon leprechaun, knocked his heels together once, and kept running.

Kristin Reed

It's always during the last twenty minutes of that tape that the collision of stories becomes a merging or a deflection. Or an illusion, like the long shadow of a child shortening and disappearing underfoot as she runs beneath a streetlight. The reason for the ex-lover's silence on the Cowboy Junkies' tape could be a different truth in any number of stories because a fiction writer is like that real pervert. As I walked home afterwards, I told myself different stories about what had just happened. Not one of them was this one and none of them was true.

D. H. CARLEY

D. H. Carley lives and writes in Sointula, British Columbia, and has been published by the *New Quarterly, Other Voices, sub-TERRAIN,* and *Women's Press.*

Benny Got a Gun

EVERY
DAY IT'S THE
SAME OLD BORING
SHIT. GO TO WORK EACH NIGHT IN A

STINKING HOT LAUNDRY, COME HOME EARLY IN THE

morning, wander around the apartment, the sounds of the rest of the world buzzing in my ears until I can't keep my eyes open no more. Then I close the curtains, unplug the phone, put on my sleeping sunglasses, and hope some fuckstick with a mission from God don't decide to ring my bell and share the word.

And I sleep, a couple of hours at a time, a murky muddled sleep. I can barely remember what it's like to wake up without my mind all bloated. Every afternoon, my whole fucking body is thick and sore like I been stuck for a week under the rubble of a three-storey house after a quake.

I'm good and ready for something choice to happen when along comes my boy to make everything all right. We meet by chance me and him. Saturday at three in the morning, I'm at work, sorting through stuff that's come in from the hotels downtown, when something drops out of the smelly pile of sheets and clanks against the cement floor. Nobody's looking so I scoop him up, shove him under my smock, and act like I don't know nothing.

It's not so unusual as you think for something to drop out like that. You'd be surprised what comes in rolled up inside linen and towels and tablecloths. Most of the stuff you find ain't liable to be looked for neither. If it was something needed hiding, not many's going to be coming around making a big fuss looking for it if you know what I mean.

It doesn't completely hit me what I got, till I get him home and pull him out. He fits in my hand so nice. I love the feel of his smooth ivory handle, lean round muzzle, my finger rubbing against his curved trigger. This could be the beginning of a beautiful relationship.

God knows I could use one. Ever since I started working night shift at the laundry, I've been out of synch with the rest of the world. What kind of life can you have when you're upside down from everybody else?

Not that this girl wants to pull a postie or nothing. My job may suck but I don't need to shoot up a bunch of people to prove my point. No, this is a private, personal thing, something between him and me. Or at least that's how it starts. But of course then I go and phone my little brother Benny, tell him I got something to show him.

Benny has this thing where he likes to play like he's a busy guy. He's got deals cooking, plans stewing; he's a regular chef of possibilities. Yeah right Benny, whatever gets you through the night. So even though he's practically busting down my door by the time I hang up the phone, he still acts like he's doing me a big fatty. As if. Two can play that game, buddy boy.

I give him a beer, don't say nothing about my new boyfriend. He tries to act like no big deal, he's too cool to give a shit, but he doesn't even come close to pulling that one off. We're sitting there drinking beer, staring at the TV, for like, a total of ten seconds, before he cracks.

Even as a little kid, he couldn't hold back. Staring contests, hide and seek, he could never keep still long enough to be found.

He begs me to tell him what I got. I pull out my beautiful boy. Benny doesn't even pretend not to be impressed.

"Oh, wow, Lucy," he says, reaching for him. "Wait'll the guys see this."

"The guys ain't gonna be seeing nothing, Benny. Give him back. He's not for you to be messing around with."

"Run for cover, Benny got a gun. Bam, bam."

"Knock it off, Benny. I'm not joking. Give him here."

"Oh sure, Luce, don't mean nothing. Boy, nobody mess with old Benny if Benny got a gun."

"Somebody messing with you?"

"Nah."

"You better not be hanging round those creeps at the centre, Benny. They're just gonna get you in shit."

He looks down at his feet, his head-banger hair hanging dirty and tangled over his face. Ragged blue jeans hang low on his hips, a black denim jacket over a T-shirt with a beer logo shining big and bright across his chest.

That boy's hands never stop moving, swinging against his thighs or flapping through the air like a sparrow with a busted wing. He's always getting in shit. So far it's little stuff, but one of these days I'm afraid he's gonna get himself in some serious shit. Then what? I never should have shown him my boy. It's just giving him ideas, and the one thing Benny don't need is more ideas. He just sets himself up to be shot down.

Like that time soon after Momma died—a fast car, Daddy driving, a tree, don't ask—when Benny didn't come home after school. I went looking for him and finally found him still in the schoolyard, laying on the grass beside a tiny patch of dirt. He didn't hear me coming or maybe he didn't care. I knelt down beside him but he still wouldn't look up at me.

I said, "What ya doing, Benny?"

He said, "I'm waiting."

"Waiting for what?"

"I'm waiting for my sunflower to grow. I put a seed in and I gotta wait for it to grow."

I figure he'd have sat there all night if I hadn't come and got him. I took him home and made him three hot dogs with lots of ketchup, just the way he likes them.

Then there was that time he was fifteen and came to me hell-bent on having a picnic at Jericho Beach. He was going through this stage where he kept trying to be like everybody else. Like he was ever gonna get there. My little brother, in desperate need of St. Jude, patron saint of lost causes and fine white sand. He wore cut-off blue jean shorts, his legs white spindly sticks with dark coarse hair below his knees like a mass of burned-up twigs.

I'd brought ham sandwiches, chips, and Coke. We were gonna have us a regular Kitsilano experience. He'd brought along a Frisbee. Only trouble was, he couldn't catch it to save his life. He was the clumsiest boy I ever seen. Oh, he tried, clapping his hands in some kind of spastic attempt at grabbing it from the air. When it smashed into his face, he scooped it up, sent it back in the air to me, as if by moving fast, he could pretend it never happened. Except for the blood gushing out of his nose. I never saw nobody try so hard to have a normal life and be so bad at it.

Good thing there's one of us in this room knows her life ain't never gonna look like the ones on TV. I give Benny another beer. Benny likes beer. I shove my guy in the top drawer of my dresser while Benny's back is turned. I throw a video in the machine. We watch the shows I tape for him every week whether he bothers to show up or not. Cops, America's Most Wanted, and 911.

Benny don't say nothing about my new boyfriend and you know I don't. We drink my beer, as always. I'm the one with the job, Benny likes to remind me, saying it like it means I just keep opening up my wallet and finding all kinds of bills stuffed inside. Like it don't involve spending forty hours of my week in a hellhole of a job that don't let me sleep nights and has me in some kind of ugly shit fog during the day.

I lean across Benny to grab a smoke. He pulls away like I was reaching for his dick. "Whoa, chill there boy, I ain't grabbing nothing of yours."

He doesn't take his eyes from the TV.

"So Benny," I says, "how's your girlfriend?"

He looks at me all confused. I blow smoke in his face. "Just pulling your chain, boy, see if you're paying attention."

He makes to leave. I jump up, pull out another beer and wave it in front of his face. He grabs it from me and sits back down. It's not like he's great company or nothing, but this is about as good as it gets for me these days.

When the beer's gone, so is Benny. I open the top drawer of my dresser and shove my hand beneath the mess of pink and blue panties. At least my boy's still there waiting for me. I pull him out, open my closet door and stare at myself in the full-length mirror hanging inside. I do my Angie Dickinson, I'm a police chick and I look fine stance, legs spread apart, both hands clutched tight round the hardness of my boy, pointing him straight between my eyes. I let my arms fall to my side, pretend I'm talking to my partner, when suddenly—a noise. It's coming from over there. I swing round, strike the pose, and damn I look good.

Okay I wouldn't be mistaken for Angie in a dark alley by a blind man pissed out of his gourd, but I'm doing the best I can for a short, skinny chick with bad skin and shoulder-length dirty-blonde hair. Like what kind of colour is that anyway, dirty blonde? You'd think somebody could have come up with a better description of the natural hair colour of half the white people I know.

I wander over to the window, look out on the street. The hookers and dealers are out in full force as the decent people get ready to sleep. You'd be surprised, though, how many respectable types come slumming down here. All these people selling, somebody got to be doing the buying and anyone that got the money to do that sure ain't living in these parts.

I start feeling like an alley cat in heat locked up inside while half a dozen toms are doing their randy moaning love song outside my window.

I've got this beautiful new boy in my life; it's time to do something new.

I call in sick to work again. Just my luck I'll get fired. Last week my boss had a little chat with me. There I was listening to Mister "I don't want to hear about you missing any more shifts" creepface Fraser, thinking, you give me any more grief, you pond scum that walks like a man, and you won't be hearing anything from those pudgy ears of yours, you ugly bonehead twit. Of course I didn't say nothing to him. I just nodded my head like he was saying something smart, something I'd be sure to remember. He sent me off with a wave of his hand, looked down at the papers on the desk, his double chin flopping over his collar like a pink fish tossed onto a beach.

I imagine seeing the muzzle of pistolboy pressed snug against his greasy temple while I say, "I'm sorry, I didn't quite catch that. Could you repeat what you said, please."

He'd shit his pants, a wuss like him, bullying girls and immigrants too scared to lose their jobs. Somebody should take him on, somebody like me and my boy.

I pull on my old sweatshirt, my favourite flannel jacket with the big pockets and shove my sweet boy inside the waist of my pants. Flicking off the light, I close my apartment door and head down the stairs.

I step outside. Shouts and sirens echo along the dark shiny street. I shove my hands inside my coat pockets feeling safe 'cause I got my boy with me. I try not to think about Benny wandering around alone, no one to protect him but me, and me not doing such a hot job of that anymore. It's not that I don't try. It's like he won't let me. Fine, that's his problem. I got enough to worry about without trying to mess around inside that boy's life.

I head deeper into the city, into the darkness. When it's not raining, this town sparkles like a postcard, like nothing could ever go wrong here, it's too sunny and bright and beautiful. But on a night like this when the skies match the street, grey and sad and dirty, I get to feeling trapped and closed in. And the fucking rain starts to feel as if it's never gonna stop, the dark wet hours sliding one into the other with no beginning and no end.

D. H. Carley

Sometimes it seems that Benny and me are stuck in a place like that, in some kind of dirty light where nothing ever seems clear or right. Yeah well, fuck Benny, I don't need him. I got me a new pretty boy and this one's gonna do me right.

I see myself in a pawnshop window. I look cool, sharp, ready for anything. And I am. Not like the rest of the cracked types wandering around vague and confused while the tourists in their slick matching khaki pantsuits act like they're visiting one of those fake frontier towns, a little show put on just for them.

When this wanker starts hitting on me, do you think I could care? Big deal. I've blown off guys like this without missing a step. Trouble is, this one's drunk enough to be brave but not so drunk that I can easily step around him. I can take care of myself, you understand, but even so, it's always nice to have a little backup, a tough boy who don't take kindly to strangers whipping around his gal.

It's enough to feel his smooth barrel against my gut, ready, waiting, until this guy gets downright pushy. He grabs at my arm. I feel his fingers digging hard and mean into my flesh. I lurch away from him, say, "Who you think you're grabbing there, bucko?" And this limp dick says, "An ugly bitch with attitude."

"Really," I says. "You ain't seen attitude like you're gonna see, asshole." He barks a laugh like I'm some kind of big joke and leans in closer. His breath is stale and dark and his grip is strong. Not this time, prick. I reach into my pants, pull out my boy and introduce him to Mr. Personality. The guy blinks like I've done some great trick he's seen but can't quite believe. He lets go of me. I give him my prettiest smile. "You were saying?"

I can see him thinking about bluffing me out but, smart boy, he decides not to bet against someone holding a full house. I let him bow out gracefully, which for a guy like that means turning tail and slinking away. I hold my boy up to my mouth, blow a kiss of breath across his tip like a sharpshooter in the Wild West who's just run the bad guys out of town. I could seriously get to like this show.

I wander around awhile, getting a kick from just being able to walk wherever the hell I want. Not too many times that's happened before. Usually I got to be looking over my shoulder everywhere I go.

I get a couple of near misses, a few guys who look like they want to mess with me. Maybe it's 'cause I'm walking differently knowing I got my boy in my pocket and no, I'm not happy to see you, but they just kind of drift off like a bad smell on a windy day before I get the chance to show them my stuff.

Then it's like I'm totally alone, there's nobody left on the streets, and all of a sudden I'm dead tired. I head home, the night quiet and dark and empty around me. Walking up the stairs, I see the door to my place open. Inside, my stuff is thrown all over the place. Benny turns and looks at me. His eyes are glassy. He's holding a ripped pillow in his hands as he moves towards me.

"What the fuck are you doing?" I yell at him.

"I'm in trouble, Luce. I . . . I . . . I need your gun."

"You've wrecked my place, you fucker."

"I mean it, I'm in some deep shit. I gotta have the gun."

"Damn right you're in some deep shit and you are digging yourself in deeper, boy."

He holds out his hand, "Give it to me, Lucy, please."

"Like fuck I'm giving it to you, asshole. Whatever kind of trouble you're in, this'd only make it way worse. Trust me."

He comes towards me. I pull out my boy and point him straight at Benny's chest. He looks at me like he did that time he was seven years old and I told him ain't no sunflower going to be growing out of that dusty piece of ground. Like my one joy in life is letting that boy down when all I do is try and save him from just that thing.

Then he runs out the door and I'm left holding my boy too hard too long like a kid still hugging her pet bunny after it's gone limp in her arms.

ALISA GORDANEER

Alisa Gordaneer grew up in
Victoria, British Columbia.
She now lives in Detroit,
Michigan, with her hus-
band and son, and works as
an editor at the *Metro Times*,
an alternative newsweekly.

The Dock

HOT
AS A BREAD
OVEN, THAT SUMMER
HUNG BEHIND OUR EYES. IT

STRETCHED WARM DAYS INTO MOSQUITO-PLAGUED nights scented with tired grass, rotting fruit, and wilting roses, the thirsty garden a nagging character in our hot-pillowed dreams.

The heat wove itself tangibly into the weft of Gramma's rag rugs, into the knotty plaits she tangled in my hair, into her braided Saturday loaves of cardamon-scented pulla. For the first time ever, we looked forward to school, to going back to the city, even to a visit from Mom and Dad. Anything to escape the baking stillness, the season of slow torture. We ached with a longing we had no name for, with a restlessness we couldn't understand.

Justin, Timo, Erkki, and I spent days on the wooden dock that floated on the river at the foot of Gramma and Grampa's yard. It had once served as winter moorage for their fishing boat, but was now used only by us kids. Grampa had refused to go there ever since the doctor said he couldn't fish anymore, and he'd sold the boat to a man who sank it in the next storm. Gramma, for her part, knew that feeling of sinking to the bottom, as she had once done, with fishing weights in her pockets and rubber boots on her feet. She feared, almost to distraction, the possibility of falling in again.

Fearless conquerors of unclaimed territory, we made the dock our own world, dangled our feet in the low water in an attempt to soothe away the parched season. Emptying just a few miles downstream into the ocean at Alberni Inlet, the Somass River ebbed and flowed around our ankles, its tides rising and falling gently, like breath. The river a cool drink, but brackish and unsatisfying.

Time swam by with the tides, but in the heat we could believe that autumn would never come, school would never start, and summer, painful ache that it was, would go on forever. Forever.

Forever was even bigger than the distance between the earth and the sun, Justin told us smugly. As the oldest, he knew everything. Forever. We used the word a lot, both loving and fearing its possibility of everything and nothing. Its power to defer the onset of September, and at the same time, the terrifying thought that it might.

Summer unrolled like the night sky, stretching over us like a smothering quilt.

One day, restless, we cut our fingers with Justin's Swiss Army knife, bleeding drops into a puddle and wincing. Before it could melt into a stain on the dock's weathered boards, we dipped fingertips, tasted. The salty metallic sting on our tongues. Now we're blood joined, Justin pronounced. Cousins forever.

We were bound. Despite Justin's teenaged mood swings, despite Timo's constant pummelling of anyone who got too close. Despite Erkki's seven-year-old youngest-kid whining. Even despite my own biological misfortune of being a girl. We ran to the house, toasted each other with overspilling Tupperware cups of sima, the bubbly raisin-filled lemonade Gramma made and kept in the fridge. The raisins went up and down in the cups, carried by bubbles.

Gramma called to us to hush up, Grampa was sleeping.

The afternoon wore on.

Flattened by the heat, we lay again on the dock, too tired to reach over the edge to splash each other, too lethargic even to start a punch-up. Justin, suddenly itchy in the shimmering air, spoke with exaggerated enthusiasm. "D'ya wanna go pick blackberries? Gramma will make us a pie." He rubbed his tummy in an exaggerated expression of hunger, licking his lips in an attempt to stir our stomachs into action.

"Naaah. It's like a sauna out. An' there ain't enough berries ripe to bother." Timo swung one foot into the river, dabbling his toes in the cool water and swinging his foot up to flick drops over himself. Justin shrugged, a reluctant acquiescence. In the dry summer, the usually lush blackberry brambles were sparse and studded with more thorns than made the few sour fruits worth risking. Even our optimistic Gramma shook her head when she returned to the breakfast table after each morning's inspection of the gardens.

"Ta whole karten is dry essa bone," she'd declared over breakfast, instructing us kids to scoop buckets of water from the river to pour on the struggling potatoes and turnips. As we sweated up and down the thumping wooden walkway from the dock, splashing more water on ourselves than on the garden, she'd pinch the soil between her thumb and forefinger, lips pursed as it crumbled away.

"Why do we hafta water the stupid plants, anyway?" Erkki whined, when we'd finally sat down for lunch. Gramma frowned as she carefully placed a rice-filled piirakka on Grampa's plate. "You wanted to haf nutting to eat tis vinter?"

Grampa grunted, a brief sharp word in Finnish, and Gramma continued. "When tere was ta War, we eated only potatoes." She took a piirakka from her own plate and put it on mine. "You growing. You needet dis more dan me." I shook my head, tried to refuse. Gramma piled another spoonful of mashed potatoes onto my plate.

"But now you can go to the grocery store, Gramma," Justin scoffed, his fourteen-year-old wisdom ignoring her. "You always have lots of food here," he shrugged, cutting a slice of pulla from the braided loaf, stuffing it folded into his mouth.

"Yust watter, and you will haf more. Now go play, your grantpa liked to sleeping."

Grampa settled on the living room couch. Gramma's worn dishtowel, printed with a blue and white map of Finland, shooed us back out into the heat.

From the dry lawn, I watched as Gramma performed her after-lunch ritual. Every day, while Grampa napped, she collected the water from last night's vegetables, the leftover steam water from the sauna, the water distilled in the tray at the bottom of the refrigerator, and poured it all into a faded blue plastic bucket. She'd lug this bucket outside, and administer it carefully to the base of a struggling apple tree planted in the corner of her garden. Standing silent, she'd watch until all the water was absorbed into the soil, and then pat the tree's slim rough trunk, caressing its grey bark. At the top of the tree, her diligent watering had resulted in a meagre crop of seven Golden Delicious apples, which ripened like miniature suns. She'd shade her eyes and look up at them, murmuring something I could never quite hear.

Justin watched as Gramma wiped her brow with the hem of her apron. "She talks to trees, y'know," he said, his eyes narrowed in a sly expression.

"Yeah, and the trees talk back to her. In Finnish. I heard them once, and I even understood them, too." I wasn't about to let my cousin outdo me. Even though he was three years older, I rarely let pass a chance to top him. He might be bigger and stronger, but I was smarter. This irked him, and I knew it.

"Shut up." His jealousy bubbled to the surface. Despite lessons, despite practice, he'd never caught more of our ancestral language than piirakka, pulla, lyyha—the words for foods. Dumplings, bread, meat.

I, on the other hand, could almost carry on a simple conversation. "Puhun suomea. I speak Finnish, and you don't! Ow! Hey, stop it!"

Alisa Gordaneer

Poking each other in the ribs, we rolled over the prickly yellow grass almost to the edge of the lawn, where concrete slabs shored up the riverbank from erosion. Not to be left out of the fun, Timo and Erkki roused themselves from their examination of a worm, leaving it to bake on a slab of rock, and joined in. We punched and rolled and yelled, piling on top of each other, pinching and tickling, until the heat folded over and we lay on the grass, laughing up to the thin, clear blue sky.

The earth turned.

The sound came quietly at first, like the buzz of a mosquito, and then built up, rising from the soil to pierce the air with a scream that rose until it suddenly stopped, an eerie suspension of time. We looked at each other, still and afraid. Gramma, her face pale and her lips pursed, came outside to tell Justin to look after the rest of us, just for a while. And she and Grampa were whisked off in a white van, its sirens howling through the hot streets.

We sat in the muggy shade at the front of the house, watching the empty place in the driveway where the ambulance had stopped, where the stretcher had been placed, where we last saw our Grampa, pale and small beneath blue emergency blankets. Silent.

We hardly dared look at each other. Justin's fingers tapped a gentle rhythm on his bare dusty knees. Timo pulled apart a small purple dahlia, petal by drying petal. I hugged my arms around myself, and Erkki began to cry. "Why can't we go, too? I wanna go with them." Tears smeared his dirty face.

"Shut up, baby. We can't, all right?" Justin assumed the power of the eldest.

"But why?"

"Because it would scare little kids like you. They'll prob'ly hafta cut him open, like they did last time. It's called open-heart surgery. Mom tole me."

"That's gross, Juss," Timo said, launching a handful of dahlia petals at his brother. The wrinkled scraps fell limply on the dirt.

Erkki's eyes teared up again. "Izzee gonna die?"

"Naah. Gramma says he's got sisu. That means he's stubborn. You know, strong." Justin's voice cracked on the word strong. Timo and I giggled despite our moods, and even Erkki grinned. Justin shrugged. "But he can't live forever, y'know. Maybe sisu runs out, too."

The word. Forever. The hot sun, the sky, the aching in my stomach. Burned onto my eyes, the image of the ambulance, pulling itself away into its wailing as the heat pulled the distance between the sun and the earth closer and closer. Forever, shrinking into that scorching afternoon.

Timo looked up from his little pile of dahlia petals. "How do you know if you have sisu?"

"If you're Finnish, you just have it," Justin sniffed, sure of his birthright. He flexed his new, growing bicep, admiring its smooth curve.

"But we're Canadians," I pointed out. "We were all born here." Annoyed, Justin glared at me as Timo and Erkki nodded at the indisputable fact: We'd all come to life in the Port Alberni Memorial, the same hospital our Grampa had just been taken to.

"Okay, so we gotta prove we have it." A sneaky grin spread across Justin's face. "You wanna try'n prove your sisu, guys?"

Timo nodded quickly, and Erkki, tears forgotten, clapped his hands. Wary of Justin's grin, I felt a prickling at the back of my neck. They looked at me, waiting. Grasshoppers cracked their wings in the heat. I nodded.

"Okay, here's what we gotta do. We gotta walk through the whole blackberry patch, the long way. In our bare feet."

"No way, Juss. That's crazy," I said, shaking my head. The patch was almost thirty feet long, dense with brambles. Only the outermost reaches were ever explored by even the most daring berry pickers. "We'll get stuck and never get out."

"Well, you don't have sisu, then. Huh. I guess girls just don't. Are you men up for it?"

Timo and Erkki nodded again, this time less quickly. Justin grinned. "All right, let's go."

They raced to the edge of the brambles, taunting me with sneers. I jumped up after them, reached the bushes before Erkki.

"Girls don't got sisu," he taunted, and started to wade through the bushes, biting his lips as the sharp thorns bit into his legs. Justin and Timo stuck their tongues out and pushed headlong through the brambles, wincing determinedly.

"Whatsa matter, Kirsti? Ya scared? Girls are chickens, girls are chickens!" Timo taunted, yelling louder than the hurt of his scratched legs. Justin and Erkki joined in, shouting "girls are chickens" instead of screeching every time a thorn poked into their bodies.

My face hot, I glimpsed their bloodied legs between the few gaps in the brambles, saw the overripe berries perched on the inner branches fall into great purple stains on their sun-bleached T-shirts. They shouted and teased, all the while making their painful, triumphant way through the bushes. I stood at the edge of the brambles, unable to will my legs to endure.

As the boys made their way deeper into the bushes, I plucked a single drying berry and ate it, its juice already fermented and moulding, a miserable bitterness. As they emerged from the other end of the bramble patch, tears made wet trails on my dry cheeks.

Justin and Timo whooped, and even Erkki stifled his anguish in an exultant shout. They hobbled down the walkway to the dock, eager to bathe bloodied legs and punctured feet in the cool river. They clapped each other's backs, punched each other's arms playfully, and splashed water, diving and swimming the length of the dock. I crept down the walkway. Sure, they'd laugh at me, but at least I wasn't bleeding everywhere.

But as I was about to set foot on the warm boards, Justin, sitting in a puddle of bloody water at the edge of the dock, shook his head. "No way, Kirsti. Yer chicken. Only people with sisu can come on this dock."

"Yeah, you can't be in the sisu club. Yer a girl!" Timo snorted. Erkki flapped his elbows in the air, clucking.

I turned and ran back up the walkway, to where Gramma had forgotten her blue plastic bucket on the grass. It was still half full of water, and a few drops splashed out onto my legs as I kicked it in frustration. I hauled it up, ready to whirl around to splash the water over the laughing boys on the dock below.

A small thud on the hard grass stopped me. I turned, looking for the stone the boys must have thrown. There was none. I looked again. Beneath the spindly tree, one perfect yellow apple lay on the drying soil.

I poured the rest of the water carefully around the base of the tree trunk and watched as the moisture pooled, then slowly disappeared into the earth. I wiped my eyes, fighting back humiliating tears.

"Tank you. You make-da tree live."

Gramma stroked my back gently, and when the tears came again, she hugged me close. "Is okay. He yust haved a little pain in his heart. But he haved sisu, he'll be okay."

At the word, I cried harder. "I don't have it," I snuffed. "I don't have sisu. They said so."

Gramma shook her head slowly, her wrinkled face hardening. "I see dose boys. They tink sisu is only getting scratchis on tere legs. But who is smarter, eh? I thinked my Kirsti has sisu, ya, because she doesn't go into bramples."

Wiping my eyes on the sleeve of my T-shirt, I remembered the small sun on the ground.

"One of your apples fell down. You should eat it."

Gramma shook her head and stooped to pick up the apple. "You eat. Te tree have sisu, too. It maked you strong." She held the fruit out, her bent hands shaking, her face a sudden smile.

"Or maybe you take for your teacher on Montay, ya? School commet soon."

The fruit cradled between my palms was warm, a golden orb that smelled sweetly of apple, its smooth skin touched with moist earth. I held it close to my nose, my lips. To bite was unthinkable. I held it for a long time after Gramma went back to the hospital to see Grampa again, and for a long time after the boys ran to the park to play without me in the cooling evening.

I only cried because I wanted to eat the apple. And because I wanted, forever, to hold that golden sun in my hands.

JOE ABERNETHY

Joe Abernethy lives in Chilliwack, British Columbia. His writing has appeared in *Geist*, and "The Terminal Canopy" was first published in *Smallprint*.

The Terminal Canopy

THE
BOAT WAS
NOW IN THE TERMINAL
AND THE CROWD WAS GROW-
ING HYSTERICAL. RON LOOKED UP AT THE SUN, shielding his eyes with his hand. A thick wave of nausea rolled through him. He retreated under a large canopy to shade himself.

The terminal was located in a small village on the coast. The village resembled many others along the coastline, only this was the last he would visit. Many travellers ended up here at the end of their trip as the terminal was the only one with a boat that sailed the long journey up the coast, enabling passengers to return to their homeland.

He had been travelling for many months, but his voyage had yet to assume the sort of higher meaning that he felt was, after all, the true objective of travel.

He travelled alone. When alone, he had always believed, one could experience personal revelation—as opposed to those he watched around him, whose trip was shared by a spouse, or friends, or family, and in such cases there could be no element of surprise. From the commencement of his trip he had insisted that the purpose of travel was to escape the familiar.

But on this final leg of his journey, he was weakening in his convictions. *Perhaps it is foolish*, he thought, *to suppose that anything much can happen at all when one is alone.*

The canopied area faced a sandy beach. A long dock stretched from the beach out into the water to the waiting ship, which shimmered white in the heat.

Nearby was the village, including a few shops of no interest to Ron, and an outdoor bar that he had noticed upon his arrival was named "The Red Umbrella." He had considered sitting down for a drink, but feeling ill from excessive sun he headed straight for the shade of the canopy.

He watched the giant boat through the haze of dry afternoon heat. The trip up the coast would be a long one. There would be no stopping.

There was excitement around the terminal. Children screamed and ran around parents, and parents spoke to friends, who spoke to their friends, who often laughed. He watched a young father chase a toddler across the sand. The child ran with his head tilted back, gleeful bursts exploding from his wide-open mouth. Beside Ron, a man and woman lay on a blanket, embracing with eyes closed, their features tanned and satisfied. A brown-legged teenage girl performed vigorous jumping jacks on the beach, impervious to the sun's raging heat. Her feet threw small clouds of sand into the air.

Since the arrival of the boat the crowd had engaged in a steady, unceasing conversation. Ron let his head droop. He had no choice but to listen silently.

Hard to believe, he thought, *that I am one of* these *travellers.* He was indeed impressed by the fact that everyone at the terminal waited for the same boat. He could, if so inclined, approach any one of them and say, "Excuse me, are you waiting for the boat that will take us up the coast?" They would respond, beyond any doubt, "Yes, I am." *Unless,* he considered, *unless possibly he asked a child.* A child instead of answering him might cry and run to a parent, a parent who could speak for him: "Yes, I am," they would say, the child cowering behind a plump and bronzed leg. They could speak naturally and honestly. This confidence impressed him; he did not feel qualified to express such certainty. His own trip had been such a rotten failure.

He grew nauseated again and buried his face in his lap. He ran his hand through his hair, bleached almost white from months in the hot climate. His pale, baby-like skin had acquired a deep blush. He lifted his head slightly and scratched a crimson arm with his fingernails. Tiny flakes of dead skin gathered on the surface. He continued to scratch until his entire forearm was veiled in white residue, then blew on it softly. Dry flakes drifted peacefully onto the sand beneath him. He began to repeat the process on his other arm, but was interrupted by a female voice.

"You are sick?"

He looked up. She was likely closer to middle age than he, but quite good-looking. He was not disappointed by her interruption.

"Yes," he said. "Everyone's going mad here and the sun is very hot."

"Yes," she said. "The sun is very hot and life is also very horrible."

The woman remained standing while she spoke. He noticed there was something peculiar about her arms. The sleeves of her long shirt fell like perfect cylinders down each side of her torso, terminating just below waist height. He thought this bizarre and followed the length of her sleeves with his eyes. He was bewildered in finding no hands visible at the sleeves' ends. She shifted her feet and one sleeve swung forward like a pendulum. He observed this unnatural motion and it occurred to him that this woman had no arms. It was as if each arm had been shorn off, shoulder and all, by a giant pair of clippers.

The woman nodded. "You see I have no arms."

His realization had not arrived gracefully. "You don't," he agreed.

The woman spoke with a slight accent, but he could not determine its origin. Her face, though, he had to admit to himself, was very nice. Yet he couldn't help adding inwardly, *She has no arms.*

"You travel alone?" she asked.

"Yes," he said. "I prefer to travel alone. I prefer to experience things. . . ." He paused and then repeated, "alone."

"I am also travelling alone," she said. "Life can be very horrible in that way."

He nodded despite his assertion that he preferred such a manner of travelling.

The woman did not avert her eyes from him while they spoke. He noticed that her eyes were set wide apart, but not to a degree that made her look simple. Rather, it lent an exquisite sense to her and, aside from that, he found he could look into both her eyes at once, which he had observed in the past was usually an impossible thing to do. *Yet, she has no arms,* he thought. And then: *She has no arms, but to what detriment?*

A nearby child began to bawl. It put its head back and screamed for its mother, who was apparently elsewhere.

Ron cringed at the child's piercing voice.

"But of course," the woman said, "you are feeling ill. So I should let you be."

"No, no," he said quickly. In fact, he did still feel queasy, but far preferred this circumstance to merely enduring the ever-growing frenzy of the crowd.

The child continued to cry, wailing, "Mummm-y!" Others seemed to feed off the child's anxiety. A man and woman argued. The woman poked the man in the chest repeatedly. "You're hurting! Hurting, hurting!" she said, emphasizing the words with each thrust of her finger.

Ron could feel the sun burning his skin despite the canopy over-head. He watched the screaming child unite with a young woman. She picked up the boy in her arms and walked away. Then she turned back to him, slowly shook her head, and carried on in the opposite direction. He looked quickly to the armless woman to see if she had witnessed these actions, but apparently she had not for she continued to watch him intently.

She sat down beside him. The ends of her sleeves touched the sand. A handbag she had balanced between her neck and what might have been a shoulder slipped and toppled onto the sand.

He considered the oddity of this woman's carrying a purse while possessing no arms to make use of it. Immediately, though, a sense of duty arose in him; he felt guilty for his initial confusion. He attempted to retrieve the purse.

"No," she said. "It is fine for now." She resumed staring at him with her broadly spaced eyes. "Have your travels been good?"

He began to nod, but reconsidered. "No, actually. I've been very disappointed with my trip."

"Yes," the woman said. "Life is often horrible in that way."

"Very little happened," he continued, "that was not ordinary." He gestured with his hand toward the crowd. "Or like all this."

At that moment a great burst of laughter erupted from the crowd.

"Indeed," she said. "This is all quite hard to bear. I find life to be an absolutely horrible thing."

"Why?" he asked, as if hearing her for the first time.

"Because," she said. She shifted in the sand to face him more directly. "It is because in life I find one can only expect impossible things."

"Like perhaps . . . ?" He suggested what he meant to say by pointing to one of her empty sleeves with his chin.

"No," she said, smiling for the first time. "Such a thing is quite possible, for it has happened. I find it less believable that this ship will ever leave the terminal. That I find a harder thing to believe."

"It will go," he said and smiled. "I'll be on it."

The woman looked at him skeptically. "Have you made arrangements?"

"Of course," he said. "Haven't you?"

"Yes," she said. "Many of them I have made. Others not yet."

He could not reply: nausea surged through him like an electric current. He scrambled to the outward edge of the canopy and vomited powerfully onto the sand. Several people turned and looked at him. Someone said, "Disgusting."

He spat, wiped his chapped lips with his arm, and kicked sand over the vomit. He returned to the woman's side.

"I'm sorry," he said. "It's the sun."

"I know it is," she said.

Again he bowed his head toward his lap and stroked the back of his scalp.

The woman shuffled her body across the sand toward him. She did so with surprising ease. Leaning close to him she said, "It is all right now, is it not?"

He nodded, grateful for the attention. She remained close to him. For a moment he thought he could feel her hand stroking his back and was briefly comforted by the sensation. He then realized that such a thing would be impossible, and he ceased to feel it.

"It has been disappointing travels for you," she said. "For me, too, there have been bad travels. And now there are only a few arrangements to be made."

"What could possibly be left?" he asked. "The ship is leaving quite soon."

"Many of the arrangements, I am sure, have been made now. But a few things remain."

"What?" He began to feel agitated, wondering if he had forgotten something himself. He found it difficult to concentrate on the matter, as the crowd had grown noisier.

The woman stared at him with great intensity. "I would be very grateful," she said, "if you could help to make the final arrangements."

"Yes," he said without hesitation. "I'd be glad to." *After all*, he considered, *she is very pretty, and, after all, a woman without arms surely does need help from time to time.*

"That is very good," she said. "But first you must go to the village. Have a refreshment. The sun is very hot and you have been sick. And perhaps it will help you in making your final arrangements."

"But I have none to make," he said.

She shook her head, which gave the effect of a hand waving in dismissal—but of course, this would be impossible.

"The boat is leaving quite soon," he said. "It is the end of my trip. I don't want to be left behind."

The woman smiled. "Of course not. It is the end of your trip. Perhaps it will be finally improved."

He nodded in submission, somehow flattered by the woman's insistence.

"You will meet me on the boat after boarding," she said. "There will be a message for you regarding the room where you will find me."

"A room?" He had not considered this possibility.

"Yes," she said. "All arrangements cannot be made otherwise. Please, take my purse, while I attend to final matters."

He nodded as if he understood. He picked up the handbag that had previously slipped from the woman's delicate balance. He wondered at the impracticality of her carrying a purse, but again felt guilty at the thought; a woman with no arms merely needs help from time to time.

"It is a horrible life," she said. "But arrangements can be made."

She awaited his response to this with a kind of motherly impatience; her eyes did not blink, her mouth neither smiled nor frowned.

"Yes," he finally said. "All right."

"My name is Marianne," she said.

He told her his name.

"Good," she said. "I will see you next on the boat. Have a refreshment, you need it. We have travels ahead of us now."

She left him, soon vanishing into the crowd, whose noisy activity he was grateful to escape for a while.

He flung Marianne's bag over his shoulder and made the short walk to the village.

He arrived at the Red Umbrella. Palm trees scattered the vicinity. The ground was sandy, as it was everywhere. No one was visible around the establishment except for a dark-faced bartender. *Most likely a native of the village,* he thought.

Despite the fact that he still felt the ill effects of the sun, he found he was not particularly thirsty. But the man tending the bar waited in anticipation and, beyond that, he felt it would be impolite to defy Marianne's suggestion that he have a refreshment.

The bartender was badly scarred. Half his face was nearly deformed with excess scar tissue. Ron asked him if he could suggest an appropriate drink. "For the end of my trip," he said.

"You are travelling alone?" the bartender asked.

"Yes," he said, but reconsidered. "Actually, no. Up until now, I travelled alone. I generally prefer it that way."

"It is dangerous," the bartender said, "to travel alone. I have always seen that to be true."

"I haven't experienced that," Ron said.

"That is surprising. It is good you are no longer travelling alone."

"Yes," he said. "I've met someone."

"A lady?" the bartender inquired. He motioned to the purse hanging from Ron's shoulder. He smiled as if he had come to a great understanding, his scarred face crumpling until it became almost shapeless.

"Yes," Ron said. "She is a woman."

"That is good," said the bartender. "Much better than travelling alone."

"It is a good way to end a trip."

"The best," the bartender replied. "I have a drink for you. For the end of your travels."

All of the tables were empty and all were shaded by red umbrellas. Ron sat down at one of them. He placed Marianne's handbag on the table and lit a cigarette. No sooner had he done so than the bartender hobbled toward him with a drink which also happened to sport a red umbrella balanced on the edge of a large glass.

The bartender had obviously suffered some substantial injury to his leg as well as to his face, for he walked badly, if quickly, away from him.

The drink he had chosen looked ridiculous. It was served in an enormous glass and coloured a deep blue.

Ron felt uncomfortable and a little silly under the red umbrella. As he sipped the drink he peered around him, curious to see if anyone noticed the spectacle he had become. But the bar still had no other patrons, and he stared toward the water. He could see the hot white blur of the boat, silent at the end of the long dock. The movements of the people in the terminal he could see also, and he imagined, though aware of his foolishness, that they could be watching him.

He removed the miniature red umbrella from the glass and dropped it onto the sand beneath the table, burying it with the heel of his shoe. Having done this he felt sufficiently inconspicuous.

He sipped the drink and smoked the cigarette in turn, not minding so much the sickly sweet taste that stuck in his throat. He was badly dehydrated and the drink was at least cool.

He leaned forward in his chair, brushing sand back and forth with his shoes. He stared into the deep colour of the liquid, admiring how the sunlight refracted in the glass to produce a blue hue on his hand. He flattened a patch of sand with his foot, slowly becoming self-absorbed and establishing a kind of game out of the sand flattening. He imagined the sand was on fire and only the firm touch of his shoes could extinguish the blaze. He calmly padded out fire after fire. One fire out, and another, and another. He felt peaceful.

He held the blue drink in one hand, the cigarette in the other. Recalling that he preferred to smoke from his other hand, he placed the drink on the table and the cigarette in his proper hand. Putting out fire after fire in the burning sand, he inhaled contentedly, blowing long graceful puffs of smoke toward his shoes, as if to aid in the whole process.

For those moments it was as if only he existed; the distant canopy, the red umbrellas, and the crowd faded into vague peripheral sensations. He gazed at the inferno, dampened by each touch of his shoe. He felt truly helpful. He extended the hand that held the cigarette in front of him, over the smouldering sand, with the sole dreamy objective of beholding the limb of he who has quelled a near sand tragedy.

He was confused by what he saw. From his fingertips up to his wrist, his hand was completely blue.

He immediately forgot about his responsibility to the sand and stood up. He looked around madly, as if his true hand had been stolen and the culprit could still be in sight. But his hand was attached to his arm and was undeniably glowing a bright blue.

He now noticed that in rising so quickly from his reverie, he had knocked Marianne's handbag off the table. Furthermore, something had tumbled out of it and now lay partially buried in the sand. He pulled the object out with his blue hand, discovering it to be a small pistol. Staring at it for a moment, he tried to imagine Marianne using the weapon, then realized such a thing would be entirely impossible. He clicked open the cylinder with his thumb and found it to be empty. He looked across the sea of red umbrellas to the bartender, who appeared to notice nothing unusual and nodded politely.

He returned the gun to the handbag and buried his blue hand deep in his pants pocket. A gun is always a strange thing, he thought, but a blue hand is stranger. He had no idea how such a mishap could have occurred. He nodded again to the bartender and walked back toward the terminal.

The passengers were now boarding. He passed under the canopy one last time, following the others across the beach and onto the dock. Now so close to the boat, the crowd was aggressive; many people attempted to push their way to the front of the procession. These endeavours produced frustrated exclamations: voices taut with the stress of boarding the ship.

He made his way with difficulty along the dock. The sun reflected relentlessly off the ship's clean white surface. He felt the nausea build in him again and stroked his hair with his good hand.

A man and child walked together in front of him. He stared at the back of the man's head in an effort to control the dizziness that began to plague him once again. Suddenly the man swung around and faced him. He looked directly at Ron, but his eyes were shiny and distant. Ron stood still. He waited.

Joe Abernethy

They had interrupted the flow of traffic and others cursed and shoved their way around. The man continued to look at Ron, his eyes welling with tears.

"I'm sorry," Ron said, without knowing why.

The man's lips began to quiver as if he might cry, but with a sharp exhalation of breath he began to laugh. The man laughed, but Ron did not. The man laughed, but there was anger in his eyes.

"I'm sorry," Ron repeated.

Just then the child who had been holding the man's hand leapt at Ron's leg and bit him hard on the kneecap. He nearly crumbled as a result of the sharp pain, but felt empowered by a dire need to reach the boat. He grabbed the child by the back of the neck, pried him off his leg, leaned close to his ear.

"Watch it," he whispered. "I have a gun."

A pair of arms forcefully removed the child from his reach.

"You," the man said, pointing his finger in Ron's face. "You don't belong here." He took the child by the hand and hurried up the dock.

Ron shook his head and, swallowing his remaining feelings of sickness with a gulp, boarded the ship.

The passenger deck was so dense with travellers that he could not imagine how he would locate Marianne. As he thought this, a crewman appeared in front of him. He bowed and handed Ron a piece of paper. He bowed again, smiling enthusiastically.

"Everything, sir," he said, "is in order. Arrangements have been made." He nodded and slid back into the swarming crowd.

Ron looked at the note which had a room number on it and handwriting that only repeated what he had already been told.

Upon entering the stateroom, he found Marianne sitting on a bed, unclothed and therefore more conspicuously without arms than he would have imagined possible. Neither of them spoke. He examined her body without embarrassment. *She has no arms,* he repeated to himself. *To what detriment?* He feasted on the sight of her body. *None,* he thought. He sat next to her on the bed. He touched the back of her neck with his hand

and kissed her. As they kissed he could feel his weary, sunburned body replenishing.

Then Marianne spoke. She quickly but carefully told him what was to be done with the contents of her handbag. He said absolutely nothing about the matter, for as soon as she finished speaking she guided him down onto the bed with a hand that couldn't possibly have been there.

They had been in the stateroom for more than an hour and sat across from one another at a table. The room was simple. There was a door, which separated them from the rest of the passengers, a bed no longer made, and a table at which they now sat. He had dressed Marianne and her sleeves once again hung loosely at her sides.

On the table was Marianne's handbag and next to it the revolver, which had been the only contents of the purse. He stared into Marianne's eyes, gleaming separately in their wide-set stance. He laid his blue hand on the table next to the revolver. Outside the room, the muted roar of the passengers could be heard.

"This couldn't be," he said. "This couldn't possibly have happened." He looked at his hand, shaking his head.

"But it has happened," said Marianne. "So it can be."

She nodded to the gun as if to point with her hand, which she nearly achieved.

"Go ahead, now," she said.

He picked up the revolver from the table. He opened the cylinder with his thumb, revealing it once again to be empty. He spun the cylinder and snapped it shut. He shook his head as if to convey to the woman across from him that she was behaving in an utterly silly manner.

"Go ahead," she said.

"This gun is empty," he said.

"Yes," she said. "Life can be very horrible in such ways."

"The gun," he repeated, "is empty."

"There are few things," she said, "that one can count on. But often arrangements can be made. One must take care of such things when travelling alone."

The roar of the crowd outside the room was fading; only a few voices remained now. He pointed the gun at Marianne's head. *She is a beautiful woman,* he thought. He cocked the hammer and smiled at her. He admired the dignified placement of her eyes. *What a lovely body,* he thought. He had the urge to tell her so. He thought it might be a nice thing to tell her that he cared for her, but he remained silent. She smiled as if she understood and he pulled the trigger of the revolver with his blue finger.

He did not know for a moment if he had truly heard such an explosion, or if the fact that Marianne now had a tiny dark hole between her wide-set eyes could be, after all, an illusion. He set the gun down on the table. He could hear no sounds beyond the stateroom. Not one voice, nor a laugh, nor a scream. He turned to the door and noticed that water was seeping in from underneath. He continued to watch and the water came in faster. He returned his attention to Marianne. She still sat upright in her chair though something in her posture was terribly off balance. He found he could no longer make any connection with her eyes. *They are changed now,* he thought. And then: *It has happened. She is dead. So it has happened.*

He looked at the unmade bed. He could distinctly recall the feeling of her hands, tight on his back. It had seemed a fine way to end a trip. A manner of travelling. And all quite possible, really.

His shoes were getting damp. He stood up and hurried out of the room.

Water rose up the companionway, flowing steadily into the passenger cabin. There was no one in sight. He began to run around the ship, becoming frantic as further moments passed without his seeing a passenger. He ran as quickly as he could, splashing through the water that flowed down the stairwell. Any minute he would see the crowd that had waited with him under the canopy. He longed to find the others. But there was no one.

"Hello!" he screamed. No one answered. The water was everywhere and rose steadily. "Hello!"

Then he heard a voice and he scrambled through the water that covered his feet now, trying to locate it.

"Sir!" the voice said. "Sir!"

"Yes!" he answered. "Here I am!"

Finally a figure appeared, limping toward him. "Sir," he said. It was the bartender. He approached Ron, and held out his hand. He pressed a small, sandy object into his palm.

"Sir," he said. "You left this behind." Out of breath, he grimaced, his scarred face crumpling. "But now I leave," he said. "This ship is bottomless."

The water rose more quickly. As the two men spoke, the water had reached their knees.

"How is that?" Ron demanded.

"It always has been."

"But what about the others?"

"They have made plans," the bartender said. "There are no others."

"But what about me?" He ran his blue hand through his hair, no longer feeling the need for concealment.

The bartender turned to leave, wading awkwardly through the water now near his waist.

"You, sir," he said, turning just enough to expose the scarred portion of his face. "You, sir, made very poor arrangements."

He moved awkwardly but steadily through the deepening water, and soon he was no longer visible.

Ron looked at the sandy object that the bartender had delivered to him. It was dirty and crumpled. He carefully unfolded the fragile paper until he was able to recreate its original form. He held the small red umbrella by its wooden handle, spinning it back and forth between his blue thumb and forefinger. He was alone.

Joanna Zilsel

Joanna Zilsel was born in
Willimantic, Connecticut, in
1953. She holds a Master's
degree in genetics from the
University of British
Columbia. She currently lives
with her elderly father, two
sons, two cats, and a dog in
Gibsons, British Columbia.

"Life Is Fragile"—her first
non-scientific publication—
is based on a real incident.

Life Is Fragile

THE
FIRST TIME
I EVER SAW DAVID (GE)
CHANG, HIS LONG, LEAN BODY

WAS LYING FLAT ON ITS BACK IN THE FUNERAL parlour on East Hastings. I was fifteen at the time, and I couldn't take my eyes off him. Adrienne hadn't been exaggerating about his good looks. "My new tenant is *gorgeous*," I'd overheard her telling my mother a few months earlier. "A face to die for!" Those were her exact words.

The thick black lashes of his closed eyes reached almost to his cheekbones. His nose was strong and straight, his full lips perfectly formed. I slowed down and turned my head to keep looking as we filed past the coffin.

To be perfectly honest, I had gone to the funeral strictly out of curiosity. I'd never seen a corpse before. But sadness overwhelmed me as soon as I arrived. The parlour itself was small and dingy—the sort of place where only folks with no money end up when they die. At least fifty people were crammed in there that morning, almost all from the university. And not one of them really knew David. I can say this with certainty, because the reverend—who acknowledged during the short service that he had very little information to go on—asked for words of remembrance from anyone who cared to share them.

One student stood awkwardly just long enough to say that David was really smart and a hard worker, "but not much of a talker."

Another volunteered that he sometimes had dinner with David— Chinese take-out. "We ate right at the lab bench. . . . If we talked . . . well . . . we talked shop."

"One of the most promising students I've ever had," a fiftyish prof offered. "A tragic loss."

The room was silent for quite a while. I was waiting for Adrienne to say something. She must have chatted with David in her kitchen now and then, but I guess she just didn't feel comfortable speaking up at the service. The reverend began to shuffle a bit at the podium—I think he was getting ready to begin his wrap-up—when an elderly Chinese woman with permed black hair rose slowly from her seat. In careful English she explained that she was David's aunt. She had come up from California for the funeral. "I never got a chance to know David," she said, her voice breaking. "My husband and I moved to the States before he was born. The first time I saw him was at the L.A. airport. I met him there when he flew over from China last September." She took a deep breath and looked around the room. "He was my sister's only child." Another word began to form on her lips but she swallowed it, lowered her eyes, and crumpled into her seat.

That was when the reverend indicated that we should move to the front for the viewing. The lineup headed straight past the coffin to a side door which opened onto an East End parking lot. I could see it drizzling outside. The reverend positioned himself beside the door and shook people's hands as they exited. Just before I reached him, I stepped to one side. No one paid any attention, so I made my way back to the coffin. The last few mourners—fellow grad students from David's laboratory, I guess—were still filing past. I walked behind them really slowly and lingered a bit after they'd gone.

The undertaker had dressed him in a formal black suit and tie, but I pictured him in a T-shirt, jeans, and old runners. Adrienne told me later that's exactly what he usually wore. He was uncommonly tall for a Chinese man—over six feet—and his hands, which the undertaker had placed clasping each other about waist-level, seemed huge. I tried to imagine them holding test tubes and the like, which is what I figured he did in the lab, but I couldn't quite get it right in my mind. And then, out of the blue, I got this really clear picture of those enormous hands holding mine. It was more than a picture. I could *feel* it—a warm, gentle squeeze.

At the time my hands were actually in the pockets of my rain jacket, my left hand fingering the amethyst crystal I used to carry everywhere. I clutched it for a couple of seconds, my heart pounding fast, then pulled it out and dropped it into the coffin. It didn't make a sound. I took one final look at David's beautiful face and headed toward the door.

The reverend extended his hand toward mine. I'm pretty sure he'd seen me give my amethyst to David, so I averted my eyes. I figured he'd want to talk—ask me questions or console me or something. I just stepped outside, zipping up my jacket as I went. I decided not to wait at the bus stop in front of the funeral parlour. I knew it was unreasonable, but I was worried that the reverend might come out and try to talk to me there. How could I explain to him that I'd never even *met* David? So I kept walking. I ended up all the way at Granville before stopping at a bus shelter.

I was feeling pretty spacey. A couple of times the thought went through my mind that I was skipping school. But mainly I thought about David. About how he'd lived right across the street from me for over nine months and I'd never once laid eyes on him. Until it was too late.

"He went to the laboratory early—usually before seven o'clock each morning—and he almost never came home for supper. He seemed to live for his work, Jen, and he was *extremely* shy." That's how Adrienne explained it to me when I went to see her after school the next day.

She'd been at a meditation retreat on Saltspring Island when he killed himself. Seeing as he had no family in this country, the police drove right up the mountain to find her. She said that as soon as she saw the cop car she knew it had to do with David, and it was a good thing she'd been meditating or it would have been a lot harder to take.

She told me there was no indication of anything being amiss until the very morning she left for the retreat. She had come downstairs for a cup of tea around five a.m. and found David standing by the kitchen stove tearing pages, one at a time, from the little notebook that he kept in his right breast pocket. He held each sheet over the gas flame until it caught fire, then dropped it onto the burner.

"I couldn't believe it, Jen," she told me, shaking her head. "It was so eerie . . . with the blue flames and all. It seemed to be happening in slow motion. When I finally got my wits about me I shrieked, 'David, what in God's name are you doing?' 'Does it bother you, Adrienne?' was all he said. Does it bother me! I told him it was dangerous—a fire hazard. He just bowed his head and went to his room. My God, I knew right then that boy was not well! I should have cancelled the retreat, but it all happened so fast. . . ."

"Extreme culture shock" was the official explanation given for his suicide. I read about it in the newspaper the following morning. According to the write-up, David was born in rural northern China. His parents—both teachers—had been tortured during Mao's Cultural Revolution. An outstanding student, he finished a Master's degree in molecular biology at the University of Beijing in less than two years. The calibre of his work was remarkable and on that basis he was selected to study abroad for his Ph.D. He was twenty-two years old when, the day after Adrienne left for Saltspring Island, he stood at his laboratory bench and drank a lethal dose of arsenic. He left no note.

All I could think about was how utterly alone he had been. Painfully

Joanna Zilsel

lonely myself at fifteen, I became obsessed with thoughts of how I *might* have met him. And how, if I had, he'd still be alive. Months before his suicide, I had made a resolution to go jogging every morning before school. As with many such vows back then, I never followed through. Now I fixated on the thought that if only I had, our paths would have crossed. He would have noticed my breasts jiggling . . . no . . . we were bonded much more deeply than that. Our *eyes* would have met first. Souls connecting. We would then have seen each other regularly: he on his way to the lab, me on my early morning jog. I would have been in terrific shape. We would smile at one another. Eventually he would overcome his shyness and greet me. One day he would notice my breasts. . . .

I dreamed about David almost every night. In one repeating dream we stood next to each other on the outskirts of a small wood. He would reach over and give my hand the same gentle squeeze that I'd felt the day of his funeral. Exhilarated, we would run down a path to the sea, holding hands and laughing. In my dreams, and often in my day-dreams, David would whisper, "Life is so beautiful now."

My social life, which had never been terrific, deteriorated completely. I closed in on myself. My mother worried a lot, but I assured her that I wasn't unhappy. And it was true. I managed to keep my grades up at school, but mostly I painted. Sometimes portraits of David. Often his hands. Sometimes landscapes which I imagined he looked at and admired. The truth is, the real world increasingly appeared to me in shades of grey.

Towards the end of my final year of high school I got accepted at an art college in Ontario. My mother was thrilled. I wasn't. My future meant nothing to me. I decided to go only because it meant I would be able to devote myself to paintings of and for David.

Adrienne came around to see me the day before I left. She smiled warmly when I opened the door. "College, eh . . . where's the time gone, Jen?" Then she stared down at her shoes for a couple of seconds. She was hugging some books to her chest. When she lifted her head she handed them to me. "You know, David's aunt came to my place after the funeral to pack up his things. She didn't bother with these. Said they were too heavy to ship, and besides, his parents don't read English. I was going to take them over to his lab—thought someone there might find a use for them—but I never got around to it. They're textbooks. Look pretty technical to me. . . . Anyway, I thought you might like to have them."

Books—four of them—that David had held in his hands, I now held in mine. I was speechless. I just nodded at Adrienne and went up to my room. They *were* pretty technical: biochemistry, statistics, microbiology, genetics. I began to leaf through them slowly, page by page. I couldn't really focus on the contents. Most of it was right over my head. Here and there I came across an underlined word or sentence, and I found a few pages with pencilled notes in the margins. Knowing David had pored over these books—that they had been meaningful to him—mesmerized me.

As I reached for the genetics text a torn piece of white notepaper, barely protruding from the top of the book, caught my eye. Several Chinese characters had been penned gracefully across it. The marked page contained an extraordinary black and white photograph. At first glance, I thought it must be some sort of fabulous blossom: nine immaculate, diamond-shaped petals radiated out from a perfectly round center. Three interconnected oval rings rested, at a slight diagonal, across each petal tip. It was spectacular. I read the caption:

Electron micrograph, magnification ca. 160,000X showing mammalian centriole in cross section. Spindle microtubules originate from centrioles. The spindle moves the chromosomes during cell division.

I examined the photograph again, trying to get my bearings, then slowly flipped the page. Another photograph: an exquisitely delicate fern-like structure curved gracefully in a field of small rosettes. The caption read:

Free polysome in cytoplasm of a chick embryo nerve cell. Magnification 31,200X.

The following pages contained more photographs: an intricate maze, swirling filaments, honeycombed matrices. All were highly magnified.

All were photos, I read, of organelles—the almost unfathomably miniscule inner components of cells. Our cells. Each with its own function. Flawless. Superb.

When I looked up from that book the world, for the first time in a couple of years, seemed alive. I wanted to run into the street, waving the photos in the face of every passerby. Wanted to shout, "This is what we're made of!" Wanted to kiss my mother's shoulders, hug our landlord's ample belly, run my hand over the school janitor's tired face. This is what we're made of!

As soon as I got to Toronto I found someone on campus to translate David's note. "Life is fragile"—that's what he'd written. I wept for days.

Last week I went to a copy shop and had the organelle photos enlarged. I tacked them to the ceiling of the small room I'm renting here. I lie on my back and study them. Lately the whole world seems different. Clearer. Vibrant. For this unexpected gift I am grateful to David Chang, who devoted his short life to the study of such beauty. Though he failed to recognize the magnificence of his own, I have, through him, begun to see it everywhere.

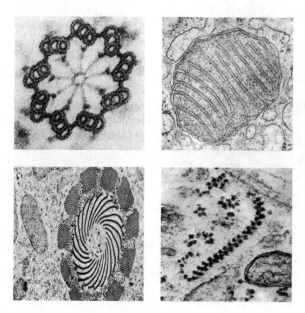

TERENCE YOUNG

Terence Young lives in Victoria, British Columbia, where he teaches creative writing and English to high school students and co-edits the *Claremont Review*, a literary magazine for young writers. His fiction has appeared most recently in *Grain, Prairie Fire,* and *Event,* and his first collection of poetry, *The Island in Winter,* published by Signal Editions in the summer of 1999, was shortlisted for the Governor General's Award. His first collection of fiction, *Rhymes With Useless* is due out in Fall 2000 from Raincoast Books.

Fast

SARAH
AND JERRY WERE
MEETING AN INVESTMENT
COUNSELLOR, BUT IT WASN'T A BIG

DEAL. JERRY TOLD SARAH TO LOOK AT IT AS A COUPLES thing, an evening with the neighbours. A welcome wagon, glad you moved in, hope you feel at home, let's drink a little wine and get pissed kind of thing. The money stuff was just an excuse. That's how Jerry saw it. Money's what you needed to do things. You didn't make plans about it. You earned it, you spent it. Anything else was taking it too seriously, too much what other people did, people who took *themselves* too seriously.

They were living in the city, then. They'd just rented the upper two floors of a house on the east side near the Italian coffee merchants and the Vietnamese fruit and vegetable vendors. Each day they took the bus up Tenth to the university, where they'd gotten jobs a few months earlier. Sarah was working in awards and loans, and he serviced photocopy machines. They sat in on lectures, sometimes went to readings. It was like being students again without the coursework. Campus daycare was the best in the city. Things couldn't be better.

It was Sarah who had answered the call from the neighbours. Jerry'd gone to the market to pick up a few things. A box of beer, a jar of peanuts, diapers. When he got back, she told him Mrs. Underwood had asked them over for dinner.

"She said she wants to break the ice," Sarah said. Their daughter Anna hung in the doorway, her feet pounding the linoleum under the Jolly Jumper. She was too big for the thing, but it kept her happy.

"What ice?" Jerry asked. "We met them on moving day. They watched, we worked, everybody talked. Ice all gone." He threw a peanut at Anna.

"It's a little more than dinner, Jerry," Sarah said.

"Call me Art," Jerry said. He'd poured a handful of salted peanuts from the jar and was throwing them at Anna, who bounced higher and higher with each peanut.

"What?" Sarah asked.

"The husband. I asked what his name was and he said 'Call me Art.'"

"Stop doing that, you moron. Anna's not a monkey." Sarah began to pick up peanuts from the floor around her daughter.

"Yes, she is. She's a little monkey, aren't you, Anna? Daddy's little monkey."

"You're the only ape in this house, Jerry," Sarah said. She took the jar of peanuts, put it in a kitchen cupboard, and closed the cupboard door with a bang. Like an echo, the door to the basement suite slammed shut beneath them, and moments later a car's engine wound up to a crescendo and then faded into the distance.

"So what's her name?" Jerry asked. He got up to look out the window at the disappearing car.

"Whose?"

"Mrs. Call me Art," Jerry said.

"Her name is Helen. The husband's a mutual funds dealer and she says he has a few ideas we might be interested in."

"They're Muslims, you know," Jerry said.

"Helen is not a Muslim," Sarah said. She picked up a face cloth and rinsed it with warm water.

"Not her. The people downstairs. The wife wears headgear," Jerry said. "There really is something sexy about a hidden face."

"Don't get any ideas," Sarah said. She washed Anna's hands, kissed her, and lifted her out of the Jolly Jumper. "I'm not your slave."

"Yes, but maybe we could pretend," Jerry said. "After Anna's in bed. You wrap yourself in a tablecloth."

"Dinner's Saturday, big boy," Sarah said.

Jerry had no training. Most of what he knew about copiers he'd picked up as a student. Whenever a department's machine jammed or ran out of dry ink, they called Jerry. He replaced staples, programmed student user cards, even did a little repair work if the job wasn't serious. The heavy stuff he left for company reps. Things got ugly when he couldn't fix an ordinary problem. People hovered over him while he pulled out rollers and flicked dust from sensors. They looked at their watches and rolled their eyes when other people came into the room, sheaves of papers in their hands. They talked about him in the third person. *He's working on it*, they said to someone passing by for the fifth time. *He thinks it's a belt*, one person whispered above Jerry's head. Their fear of a total breakdown was funny, but it was also pretty sad. Most of the time, Jerry thought it was disgusting the way professors flooded their classes with handouts.

"Lazy bastards," he complained to Sarah. "They're scared they might actually have to do some real teaching."

He disliked the students, too. Girls treated him like a construction worker, the next thing to a rapist. Some walked around him as though he were diseased, others as though he didn't exist. None of them spoke to him. Their boyfriends looked past him, far down the hall, as though they were concentrating on their futures, on the years of hard work and success that lay ahead for them, so obviously smug that they wouldn't end up like Jerry. They'd never be just some guy who ate his sandwich in the copy room sitting on an overturned recycle box. Sarah said it was his imagination, that he was judging himself.

"Those kids are too preoccupied with their own lives to think about yours," she told him. "Don't be so paranoid." She asked him to remember what it was like when he was a student himself, a whole four years ago now. Did he ever think of people that way? Did he think less of people just because they worked in a job like his? But Jerry said he couldn't remember.

Still, he was pretty much his own man. He worked everywhere on campus. They'd given him a pager, but a lot of the time nobody called. Some days he spent a few hours in the stacks, flipping through periodicals, following an idea he had. There were certain secretaries he could flirt with, too, a few even younger than Sarah. He'd ask to use the phone, and then while he was on hold to Xerox or Canon, he'd talk to them about their weekends, find out if they had kids. Pretty harmless fun, most of it, but with a couple of them, he sensed there was more than just chat going on. There was one, a temp with long black hair that she kept in a loose ponytail, the kind of hair Jerry imagined gypsy women might have, thick and full of curls. She was always putting her hand on his arm when she was speaking to him, the way some people do when they're making a point, but she left it there longer than she had to. At least, that was Jerry's impression. It wasn't as though he had timed her or anything. It just seemed long. Sometimes, too, when he asked her for something, paper to test a copier that was running low, say, she held off handing it to him right away, keeping whatever it was, paper, the phone book, tucked up against her chest until he actually had to look her in the eyes and ask for it again. Jerry told himself he'd been watching too many bad movies, but, still, he wondered what it would feel like to have something to hide, something big like an affair. In those terms—affair, adultery, infidelity—the idea seemed impossible, even ludicrous, but when he imagined just going for coffee or maybe a beer, just talking to someone different, it didn't seem so bad.

One night, he had a delicious dream. He was in a large old house, something like a Victorian brothel. Naked women walked in and out of

Terence Young

rooms, but instead of sex, they were offering him food, exotic meats and vegetable stews, the spices in the air flooding his nostrils. They wanted him to lie down and open his mouth. They stood waiting with spoons in their hands. Jerry reached out for one of the women and the movement woke him up. For a second he was sad. Then he realized he could still smell the food. At first he thought he'd left something in the oven, maybe a pot on the stove, but when he got up to check, the oven was off and the elements were cold. Still, the smells of cooking permeated the apartment. He looked at the kitchen clock: two-thirty.

"What's that smell?" Sarah asked him when he came back to the bedroom.

"It must be the people downstairs," Jerry said. He got down on the floor and pressed his ears to the carpet. Sarah joined him. Up through the joists came the sounds of pots being shifted, an oven door opening and closing, taps running. They went to one of the hot air vents and breathed in: bread, unmistakably, and a roast, the heavy scent of cumin, too.

"What are they doing down there?" Sarah asked.

"Eating," Jerry said.

"I don't think I can sleep with all that food cooking," Sarah said.

"So don't sleep," Jerry said, still aroused from his dream.

"You are such a pervert," Sarah said.

The next night, the same thing happened. They went to bed and woke up around two or three, lured out of their sleep by the aromas seeping into their apartment from below. By the third night, Jerry found he was growing fond of the idea of bed. As long as he'd eaten well himself, the smells didn't bother him, and he liked the idea of all that industry beneath him, as though elves were at work preparing dinners for poor shoemakers. Making love seemed more erotic, too, perhaps because of his dream, but also because the waves of spices and steaming animal juices that floated into their room invited a response in kind, a sensuous answer. Anna started sleeping through the night, and she seemed happier the next day, more willing to walk into the daycare and leave her parents behind.

In the office of one of the university residences where Jerry serviced a coin-operated copier, he saw a sign that instructed all Muslim students on how to apply for a cafeteria rebate during the month of Ramadan. He asked one of the staff what it meant and she explained that Muslims fasted from sunrise to sunset during the ninth month of their calendar.

"But they can eat in between?" he asked.

"Yes," she said, "but we can't stay open just for them."

"You're not Muslim, are you?" Jerry asked.

"Christ, no," the woman said. "Do I look like one?"

"Just asking," Jerry said, and then he went to the library.

"And they all do this?" Sarah asked Jerry when he told her.

"All except pregnant women, the insane, and people suffering from terminal or life-threatening diseases," Jerry recited from memory. "There are a few other exceptions, such as prepubescent children, but otherwise everybody."

"How come I've never heard of it before?"

"How many Muslims do you know?" Jerry asked.

They sat together on the couch while Anna pulled tissues from a box of Kleenex. It was cheap entertainment and they loved to watch her so happy.

"What's the point?" Sarah asked.

"What's the point of any religion?"

"No," Sarah said. "I mean the spiritual point. Is it humility? Purity?"

"Millions of people," Jerry said, " starving themselves while we're sitting here, and then getting up in the middle of the night and eating like crazy? That's not humility. That's nuts."

"Do you think our Muslims share the cooking?" Sarah wanted to know. "Do you think they have an equitable, Western relationship?"

"I've seen the back of her head twice," Jerry said.

"Let's say they do," Sarah said.

"I could never make myself get up that early," Jerry said. "And who wants to look at a pot roast at two in the morning?"

"If you believed what they believe, you'd do it," Sarah said.

Anna had discovered a second box of Kleenex. Jerry thought about Saturday and their dinner with the Underwoods. Their lives were changing. They used to visit friends. Then, they started visiting couples. Lately, it was couples with kids, and now they were having dinner with money managers. Once, when another Adventure Playground seemed more than he could bear, they had taken Anna to a cemetery by the sea. Jerry'd found a dead Sarah, and then a dead Jerry. They'd taken pictures of each other beside their namesakes. They'd taken pictures of Anna peeking out from behind a broken headstone, grey November waves breaking behind her. Children at the daycare invited Anna to birthday parties. Birthday parties meant presents and videos and return invitations. Return invitations meant party favours and goody bags and more videos. Jerry felt silly at first. He'd felt that he and Sarah were playing house. Now, he didn't feel silly at all. He felt he was slipping away.

"I wish we had something we could do together like that," Sarah said. "It sounds romantic, like it's just the two of them against the world, down there in the middle of the night, helping each other stay faithful to God."

"Allah," Jerry said.

"Don't you think it's inspiring?" Sarah asked.

"I'll bet they cheat," Jerry said.

"Cheat?"

"Sneak a sandwich," Jerry said. "A bag of chips."

"Never," Sarah said.

It was getting dark. Kleenex tissues covered the floor in front of them, a sea of paper whitecaps. Jerry got up and waded over to Anna. He plucked her from the mess and held her high over his head.

"What *is* a mutual fund, Anna?" he asked. Anna drooled a long thread of spittle onto his nose.

"That's your first question Saturday night," Sarah said.

Helen Underwood cleared away the dessert dishes. An inverted flying saucer hung above the dining room table, its halogen bulb dimmed to complement the candles still burning after two hours. Jerry and Sarah's bottle of Chilean red, freshly uncorked, sat on the buffet. Sarah had moved her chair to face Arthur, who was explaining the benefits of dollar cost averaging. Jerry tried to listen, sipping frequently from his glass.

"The idea is to think long term," Arthur was saying. "This is not some get-rich-quick scheme." He pointed at two contradictory lines on a graph.

"But still . . ." Sarah said.

"Exactly," Arthur said. "You end up miles ahead of any savings account."

They'd arrived shortly before eight, Anna ready for bed, dressed in her pyjamas, teddies and bottles tucked into her night bag. The Underwoods had insisted they bring her. They kept toys around for occasions just like this, leftovers from their own children.

"After all," Helen had said, "this is more about her than about you, isn't it?" Jerry and Sarah had agreed.

They'd spent some time walking through the house, talking about the neighbourhood, the schools. There was a Montessori only a block away, great for artistic children. The Underwoods collected art. Paintings hung everywhere, local work, not because it was an investment—although nobody could dispute the returns—but because they liked it. They liked art, they liked helping young people, they liked children. It was as simple as that. Arthur was liberal with the bar, too. They'd had sherries before dinner, two bottles of wine during the meal. Next door was not far to drive, Arthur had pointed out. He was careful to fill their glasses whenever they fell below half. Sarah had asked for soda water after a while, but Jerry kept drinking. He wasn't drunk, but he was getting there. At one point, he'd asked where Anna was. Sarah had given him a dirty look. She told him he was the one who had put her to sleep in the Underwoods' bedroom. Didn't he remember how he'd lain down on the floor beside her and drifted off himself? Didn't he remember her coming and getting him? Jerry slapped his forehead as though he'd just locked his keys in his car. He covered his glass with his hand and made the sign of the cross. Arthur laughed and filled the

Terence Young

glass anyway. Now the thread of what they were saying eluded Jerry completely. It was better to say nothing.

"Self-directed if you want," Arthur said, "though I wouldn't recommend it at first. The thing you want to do is leverage and let it build for a while. Then you can start shuffling things around."

Earlier that afternoon, Sarah had told Jerry to have an open mind. They'd gone to the dog park so Anna could watch the owners throw Frisbees and tennis balls for their pets. Anna liked to pet the smaller dogs, got excited when her favourites showed up. A stand of poplars divided the park from the busy avenue, and the city had implemented a public vegetable garden for low-income families. Couples were busy turning over soil, raking up dead leaves and weeds. If Jerry squinted, he could almost believe he was in the country except for the traffic noise. They walked the perimeter of the park. Money was a necessary evil, Sarah had said to him. She wanted a house of her own, maybe even another kid. How did he think they were going to manage that the way things were now? She asked him to tell her what he wanted. Could he at least tell her that? But Jerry couldn't. He couldn't say. How do you tell someone you're not interested in building anything together, that if you think at all, it's about having sex with somebody else? Money, houses, families, they weren't even in the ballpark. He'd tried being evasive, talked about the risks of investing.

"These guys aren't doing us any favours," he'd said. "There's always something in it for them."

"I'm not saying there isn't," Sarah said. "There's something in it for the banks, too, but I don't hear you complaining about them."

Finally, she'd told him simply not to screw things up. She'd told him not to pull his usual trick of drinking and disappearing.

"So, where exactly does our money go?" Sarah asked.

"A thousand places," Helen said. "That's the beauty."

"Who's it hurting?" Jerry asked. He hadn't meant to say it. It was something he was thinking to himself, but somehow it came out.

"What do you mean, son?" Arthur asked.

Sarah said, "He means are we contributing to child labour or destruction of the rainforest."

"You can't breathe these days without doing *some* damage," Arthur said. "The portfolios will tell you what you want to know about that."

The sound of Anna's crying drifted down the stairs to the dining room. Jerry excused himself. He'd take care of it, he offered. Sarah gave him another look.

"Don't fall asleep again, Van Winkle," she said.

Jerry turned the corner toward the stairs. He was thinking how easy lying was when people trusted you. He climbed the steps to the second floor. Anna was sitting up in bed, crying and holding on to her blanket. He picked her up.

"Hey, sweetheart," Jerry said. "Did you wake up?" He held her to his chest and walked around the room. "Did someone leave you all alone?" He swayed back and forth on his feet, rocking Anna until she became quiet.

The other day, Jerry had gone into the supplies room of the history department to get dry ink for their photocopier. It was the office where the temp worked, the one he thought of as some kind of gypsy. The supplies room was no bigger than a closet, but it was out of view of the main office, and as he was turning to leave, she came up to him and kissed him quickly on the lips. She might have been kissing him goodbye at a party or seeing him off at the airport, the kiss was that light and swift. Out of habit, he had put his arm around her waist, long enough to pull her close, as he always did with Sarah. He remembered thinking how easy it was. There'd been no walls to climb, no great chasm to cross. He hadn't struggled against competing voices in his head. It was like slipping on another jacket, as though his body had no memory of the hundreds of nights he'd slept beside Sarah. In the seconds after the kiss, he wondered what the point of marriage was if it could crumble so quickly with the touch of another person. What was the point if people were really nothing more than six-year-olds sneaking into the cloakroom when the teacher's back was turned? The woman had left without saying a word and so had he. It was just a kiss, barely that, and the slight acknowledgement he'd offered with his arm. He felt stupid dwelling on it. Sarah would probably laugh if he told her, but Jerry knew he wouldn't tell her because the invitation to return was clear. It had stayed with him all the hours in between then and now. It was why he'd held out his glass for more wine and why he'd fallen asleep beside Anna, wishing his life into oblivion. No wonder he'd slipped up at dinner, blurting out his muddled thoughts, the argument he was having in his head. No wonder he left the table to tend to his daughter. In the dining room, Sarah was planning a future for her family, and above her head he was thinking of ways to blow it to pieces.

Outside the bedroom window, a light went on in the basement of the house opposite. Jerry saw shadows move across the lighted rectangle and realized he was looking at his own house, at the basement suite where the Muslims lived. His watch read one-thirty. They must be getting up to eat. Anna had fallen back asleep. Jerry laid her on the bed and covered her up. It was probably the liquor, but everything he looked at seemed terribly strained: the stuffed animal he squeezed into Anna's hand, the bedcovers he pulled up under her chin. He was amazed how tawdry life could become in so short a time. He kissed her on the forehead and even that turned into a maudlin, tired little act.

He descended the stairs. Sarah's voice sounded angry. There was a hint of impatience rising to the surface, too.

"Look at this list," she was saying. "This is a prospectus?"

Instead of turning back into the dining room, he found himself opening the front door and walking down the steps to the lawn. Something caught his ankle and sent him sprawling. The quiet of the night fell around him and he waited to see if his fall had been noticed. Nobody came. He got to his feet and crossed through the flower bed that divided the Underwoods' property from theirs. He walked up the path that led around to the backyard until he came to the window he had seen from the bedroom. The glass was steamed with condensation. Behind him he heard Helen Underwood calling his name, and then Sarah, too. Before long all three of them were yelling for him. He put his fingers on the window's surface. He could feel the heat from the kitchen, almost smell pepper and coriander through the glass. Beads of water rolled down the misted pane in little rivers. He could make out thin ribbons of life on the other side: a beaded curtain, some fridge magnets shaped like flowers, the eyes of a girl looking out at him from a painting. Somebody crossed from one side of the room to the other carrying—what? a cat? a book?

Sarah's voice sounded closer now. Had he left the front door open? Yes, she was definitely outside.

"Jerry?" Sarah asked behind him. "What are you doing?"

"Shhhh," he said, turning to her. He'd been hoping for more time. He hadn't seen anything yet.

CATHLEEN WITH

Cathleen With is from Vancouver, BC. She is currently teaching in Seoul, South Korea and is a contributing writer for The Korea Herald. Her stories have appeared in several Canadian literary journals including the *Antigonish Review* and *A Room of One's Own.* She was a first-prize winner of the *Grain* postcard fiction competition in 1998, a delegate at the BC Festival of the Arts in Victoria, and recently won the Community Arts Council's award for emerging artists in short fiction. Cathleen is currently completing a collection of short stories entitled "Carny."

The Arbutus Tree

THERE
WAS A ROLLER
RINK OUT BY THAT CONDO
FAT-FARM WHERE OLD PEOPLE HUNG

OUT IN THEIR LONG GREY UNDERSHIRTS. "COME ON, can we, please?" we begged every night there wasn't football on the transistor radio. "No, you girls don't need to go up there and fool around like some cats in their hot heats," Mr. Coopen said, a Marlboro hanging out of his mouth.

I don't know about Tanya, but I wasn't into the creepy long-hairs that smoothed their tight Levied asses around the rinks, faces like slate stone and shifty eyes to my chest. I wanted to hear the music, slow roll to sad-crooned Cyndi Lauper, "Time After Time," and pretend I was Sheena, all-powerful, best girlfriends with Isis (second all-powerful).

"Play in the back bogland. Christ, we didn't come all the way down here to drive you shits round goddamned Birch Bay. Get outta here, go play."

She was halfway down the burnt leaves ravine before I was even at the edge. "Hey," I yelled and she turned violently, said, "Shh!", motioning for me to crouch down. I tumbled down after her, raising the dead spring beetles and chipped ladybug heads, the dead winter crap that couldn't be reached by the river runoff. "What the fuck," I whispered, and Tanya slapped out as my foot rammed into her head. She pulled me down beside her. "Look." She pointed to the overhanging arbutus branch high above us, its raw bare arms rubbing vulnerable against the tight asses of two young guys, no shirts. "Yeah?" I scoffed, turning to climb the ravine, pissed because I smelled of river muck, pissed because I was on the rag and too small to fit tampons without feeling like I was piercing my innards.

Tanya yanked me down forcefully in the bushes again. She didn't have her period yet, kept me up hours whispering in the tent trailer, her mom and dad snoozing off the beer, Timmy snoring and mumbling about rodeos. I didn't see anything up in the tree and the ravine was getting slippy under my Pony sneakers, bought only two days ago at the Fred Meyers with my own paper route money.

"Fuck you, I'm going," I said. "Look, now!" she said, mockery in her voice. I looked up to their bronzed movie star backs, no zits like Kenny from down the street who carried a knife because he thought he was tough and 'cause Danny saw his dick in the boy's room after gym and said it was little, like a dwarf's pinky. The two guys on the tree branch were necking, really giving it, I could see their tongues sliding slurpily in and out of each other's mouths, gooeying their cheeks with gobby wet saliva. "Faggots," Tanya whispered. "Cool," I said, sliding up the bank slowly, stealthily for a better look. My breathing was hard, almost like I had been running from somewhere.

Tanya's mom passed out every night we were at Birch Bay, but at least she'd stay at the campsite and not go out slopping around like my mom did at home. Summers with the Coopens at Birch Bay were supposed to be a beach getaway from the city so's your kids don't rot kind of thing. I hated sleeping in the tent trailer. Mr. Coopen, Mr. RCMP, his farts ripping over the sounds of the crows going through the garbage at six-thirty every morning. Then he'd get up and roll over Mrs. Coopen, reach down into his grey underwear and give his balls a check, scratch, and shake. He'd go outside to piss against the spruce in front of our campsite, and even though it was early and no one else saw him, he wasn't my dad, thank sweet Christ he wasn't my father.

Tanya was an intolerable sleeper-inner. I waited for her to lazily wake up, listening to the sounds of the country music station belt out from the transistor radio on the picnic table, early screeching tinny voices, and I prayed, "Please, this morning, Tanya, wake up early so I don't have to hold my pee in and wait for you." I couldn't crawl out on my own, not in the mornings, with both Mrs. Coopen and Tanya sleeping. Even four-year-old Laura would have been female protection against the Cop.

The Cop. His eyes on my pokey, too small to fit a bra, but so goddamned obvious through a T-shirt breasts. Sometimes after a few beer he'd flip the burgers, laugh, and was half decent, talking about giving good kids a break, like that program for kids he volunteers for. It sounds fairly cool, he takes them up to the woods around Squamish and teaches them neat stuff like how to rock climb, start your own fire the native way, and make a shelter with branches and leaves, shit like that. He's okay but sometimes creeps me when his eyes wander, and I'm not so sure if he's got that interested look or just that "Wow, were they ever that small?" look in his eyes. He drinks lots of Coors but never does anything. And he won't drive us to the store if he's had too many, which my mom hasn't seemed to learn.

It's hard to fucking figure 'cause lots of older guys trip on my tits. Just last week, at the PNE, in the Funhouse, the orange tunnel of vertigo part, guys at least fifteen years old I bet, six, seven of them, flicking, rubbing, and messing with me. Why can't they feel their own selves up, they've got enough to play with down in their pants.

Before Tanya wakes up, I think about crawling over to ten-year-old Timothy and putting his face in my chest. "Suck them," I would say, sexy-like, some teen throbber Brooke Shields (her mom let her do it with that guy in that tropical island movie). Timmy would grab at me gently and eagerly, like I was a full-teated cow, aching to give up her milk. Tanya rolled over to the tent flap, the canvas fabric a dead-leafed orange on her cheek. She opened one eye and said, "I dreamed about them and I wanted to almost puke, guys kissing guys." "Yeah," I said, and crawled out of the trailer tent bunk, hot from the exciting memory of it, the danger of kisses in this hick, redneck beach town.

Out in back of the campsite, down near the marshes is where we played after a cold hot dog lunch. I lost Tanya quick, she was talking to Debbie anyway, the new kid in from Skagit County in Site 18, about the faggots. Tanya was already taking lessons good from her mom and her granny and her great-granny before that. She was a gossip, my mom said, destined to become a star on the suburban housewife circuit. Tanya never wanted to play Dian Fossey on National Geo mission, or Savannah, Amazon lady of the sands of the Sahara. I knew there was more to the swampland beyond the campsites of Birch Bay. I wanted into cannibal areas, a place forbidden to menstruating women like me.

When the arbutus branches started bending downward and the spores of the plants swooped into the cups of the dewy fronds, I crouched and crawled. I made sure to seal my notebook and pencil in a freezer bag. I looked up at a branch cracking . . . and there they were. Their red, ochre-covered bodies gyrating in some tribal war dance for the calling up of crocodile spirits, their faces dripping sweat. I blinked and opened my eyes. There were no natives. Just the two guys from the arbutus branch. From the day before. On the swampy, mucky ground. Naked.

I fell to the ground, eating mossy dirt and trying to be still. There was pain on the one guy's moustached face as the other guy was moving behind him. Moustache was trying to hold back moans, but he was kind of smiling, too. The other guy was grunting like the Walker's dog Tigger last summer, when its thing was pink and he'd tried to hump everything in sight, even Mr. Walker's leg when he was sitting watching the six o'clock news. I closed my eyes and opened them again, lots of times, wondering when it would end, and if they could see me. The guys slowed and started to wind their bodies around each other, rolling, and kissing necks, chests, cheeks, nipples, so slowly, like leaves falling and resting, moss smoothed along their legs and backs. My knees were numb. I worried about Tanya looking for me, seeing them in their primal dance, and telling her dad. Would he pull out his patrolman's gun from his belt he kept in the glove compartment in the Chevy and shoot them? Calling them dirty faggots, flamers, and horrific unnaturals, like he cursed their parades he saw on the news? I wanted to warn them, whisper, "Hey, Misters, you better stop, 'cause there are people around," but I couldn't, could only watch and feel that tingly feeling down there as they caressed, rubbed each other's hair and face.

Timmy pulled me up from the sodden grassed trail later. "You all right?" he said. I whipped around to look for the two men. The spot where they had lain was bare. "What are you gawking at?" he asked. "Nothing," I said. I turned to Timmy and pulled him down beside the bracken bushes. "Hey, Timmy," I whispered. "Wanna see my tits?" "Yeah, okay," he said, smiling nervously. I closed my eyes and slowly lifted my shirt up, my tiny nipples retreating back into themselves from the slight wind coming off the bog. I leaned forward and stuck my lips on his, gummy from the Jolly Ranchers watermelon candy he sucked on. I imagined him fourteen or even fifteen and big, maybe even old enough to have some pubes. Timmy snorted from lack of air and laughed. "This is great, wait'll I tell Kenny." I leaned back into the bush and closed my eyes.

When Mr. Coopen caught us he cuffed Timmy on the side of the head, not really hard though. Timmy ran, turning around only when he got to the top of the ridge to point at me and laugh, kind of nervous-like. Mr. Coopen pulled me up and through the brush toward the campsite, through the bracken and soggy mess of the old trail, "You should know better, you're twelve, he's only ten," trying hard not to eye my breasts through the mud plastered on my T-shirt, while he held my elbow. Hard. Redneck.

It wasn't even morning when Tanya rolled over to my side, in her sleep, her body half on mine. I wanted to push her off, but I stopped, lying entranced with the sub-morning canvas-tent puke colour on her brown hair, her shirt pulled back, her neck high. My fingertips poked her almost nonexistent breasts, and I held my breath as she stirred. She fell back to sleep. I put my hand down her nightie, snaking down. I am a horrific perv, I thought, daring Tanya to wake up and call, "Daddy, Daddy, shoot her in the head, she's a horrific unnatural." Tanya was smaller than me, with hard, kind of raisiny nipples. I squeezed one and she awoke with a sleepy "Huh?" She rubbed her nipples in an unknowing itch and rolled over on her stomach.

The arbutus branch guys were at the store the last night. Me and Tanya walked up there to get milk for dinner and junk for after. She saw them first, up ahead. "See, my daddy says you can tell, by their walk." She poked at my arm excitedly. "See? There? The way that one jiggles his butt, like this." She bounced her hip against mine and giggled.

Tanya is no scaredy-cat. Right there, in that store, while I checked out the new Archie Digest, thinking whether to scoff it or not, Tanya went right up to one of the guys and said, "Where you from?" Green Hawaii shirt said, "Salem." The tank top one said nothing, asked the clerk for a deck of Lucky Strikes. "I'm from Canada, and I'm in grade seven. Are you in school anymore?" Tanya asked. "Yeah, college," Hawaii shirt said, the side of his mouth going up slightly. Then Tanya shocked me as she said, "We're going down to the beach to roast marshmallows, wanna come?" The tank top guy looked at me incredulously, and I ducked away behind the comic stand. But then Hawaii shirt said, "No thanks, honey, maybe some other time though, that'd be good for a laugh." Tanya didn't get it but smiled at me like she'd just won flirt of the year. We grabbed the bag of marshmallows, some Lik 'em sticks, Twizzlers, and the guys bought some beers. They leave and we hang back a bit after, "So we don't look too eager." Tanya said.

Timmy's looking at me when I lean down to pick out a flat one to skip. Lots of campfires, most of the kids from the sites are out. His eyes X-ray into my halter top. Mr. Coopen is drinking Rainiers, there's a stack of crushed ones beside his lawn chair, his hairy gut oozes out from under his K-Mart T-shirt. There are older boys up the beach—sixteen, maybe older, some have hair on their faces. Tanya giggles and says, "Let's sneak up on them and listen, Daddy's too drunk to miss us."

We run up the grass way and across, our feet black and hard from days of no shoes. One guy's loud and sweaty-faced, saying, "And then I poked her, did her right there beside the goddamned gym door, Mr. Carlisle didn't even see us the whole time." "Not that it took more'n two seconds for you to do her," another says. "You shut your hole," loud and sweaty boy says. Tanya starts to ease closer to their fire. "Wait," I whisper, and "Don't," but they see us and pull us into the circle. "What's here? Little girls! You want it little girls? Getting all hot listening, huh?" Tanya stands tall and says, "So who's gonna kiss me?" I slink back, horrified at her gutsiness, but loud and sweaty catches me. "Oh, we'll give ya more'n a kiss, little girl, believe me." They laugh and cackle, throw Tanya a beer, force rum down my throat. I sit on the sand and wish for Mr. Coopen to come looking for us instead of sitting drunk-enly off-duty on the same beach, half a mile down, oblivious. This isn't how it's supposed to be, isn't like the lovemaking I saw the two guys do. Tanya's screaming is different. And I couldn't get to her, my top forced up and pants down by some long-hair with Metallica on his shirt, their plastic faces ripping as I try to pull away. Tanya's cocky smile turns quickly to a grimace. Looking up from the sand, I see her face contort and pull and twist, like some Friday the Thirteenth movie, like Rosemary's fucked-up baby.

Tanya cries when the state troopers' car pulls up to the beach. The cops don't get out but the boys scatter, tripping over beer bottles and crushing cans. We huddle next to the dunes so the cops can't see us, naked and shivering. When they pull away, we quickly search the dark for our torn-off clothes, and we stagger back to the campsite. "Where the fuck were you two?" Mr. Coopen yells drunkenly from the tent trailer. "It's nearly ten-thirty!" Tanya says nothing, but looks at me with bruised wonder in her eyes. I know she's thinking the same thing I am: How did something that felt like a hell lifetime take only two hours? I climb up next to her inside the tent trailer, and we huddle inside my sleeping bag, shaking.

I had to be warrior woman, had to be strong, and the tears leaked out of my eyes as I stroked Tanya's matted hair, gently, the way I had seen the guys do down by the arbutus tree, as she whispered into my ear, "It didn't happen, it didn't happen." I murmured back to her, hummed something as she shivered, but remembered the grating of the tiny pebbles and sand against my belly, so different from what warm moss must've felt. Tanya soon dozed fitfully against my shoulder, her bruised lips resting on my neck. I couldn't sleep for a long time after.

Cathleen With

Kevin Banks spent his childhood fishing in Francois Lake, British Columbia. His first pet was a rooster named Houdini. At the age of twelve Kevin and his parents moved to Whistler, British Columbia, to live the dream. He recently completed a degree in writing at the University of Victoria and has always had a great fear of spiders, but only the big ones.

On Love and Pomegranates

SO

I'M SITTING
HERE STARING AT HER
TABLE WHILE THE ALLEGED LOVE OF
MY LIFE (THUS FAR ANYHOW) EATS A POMEGRANATE.

It's about the size of my fist. Neither of us has spoken for some time. How long, i'm not sure, but it's been a while. i'm just staring at the brown grain in the fake wood tabletop. She's eating this pomegranate; i'm staring at the table and listening to the TV. It's six o'clock. i know because the news is starting on the TV. i can see the TV over her left shoulder, when i look at her. Right now i'm just listening and staring at the table. The news is nothing new: someone's dead, the national debt is rising, they're calling for rain. i got that TV for thirty bucks at a garage sale. It's black and white, kinda flickers, but it's consistent and that's important.

She started eating that pomegranate maybe ten minutes ago. It could have been longer. There is still some juice left on the table where she smashed it to break the tough skin. And she's silent, just slurping away on the pomegranate. i'm trying to figure something out. What's that stuff they make tabletops out of? Not linoleum, but kinda the same thing. It's cheaper than wood, looks like wood, but it isn't.

It sounds like someone's moving furniture upstairs. Except that it sounds like that every day so that can't be what they're doing. i asked her once if she ever went up to ask them what they do up there. She told me she leaves them alone, they don't bother her. That's convenient i guess but i'd get sick of the noise. She used to care about stuff, now she just lets it go on and on.

The old black and white is spitting out evil commercials for paper towels, which is funny, because she is spitting pomegranate seeds into a paper towel. Its whiteness is stained pink from the juice. Why do they make them white? So you can see how much shit you mop up? i stop thinking about that and go back to staring at the arborite tabletop. Arborite, that's it; not linoleum. It almost looks real. She's done eating and i know the silence is gonna break soon.

She slams the empty pomegranate husk on a piece of paper towel and stares at me. i return a defunct gaze. She has a drop of pomegranate juice on her chin. It doesn't look much like blood but that's what i think of. Her blue eyes despise me, like the rest of her. She wants me to say something.

i just look at her. My little TV keeps babbling in the background and i keep looking at her.

i used to think she could read my mind, guess not. So i speak. "Ever been kicked by a horse?" She doesn't even smirk.

With my heart still lying on a paper towel on the table i get up and leave. i'm gonna miss that TV.

KATHRYN LeCORRE

Kathryn LeCorre was born in Victoria, British Columbia, and is currently a full-time painter and writer in Prince George, BC. She is self-taught in both disciplines, with the exception of a year's study in creative writing at the University of Victoria.

Kathryn has been published in the *Malahat Review, Canadian Author and Bookman,* and *Forte.* She recently won the top award in a juried art show sponsored by Monarch Broadcasting.

Vivaldi's Four Gynecologists

for my sister, Judy

I LOST
SEVERAL TEETH
AND TWO OVARIES THIS
YEAR, ALONG WITH MY UTERUS AND

MOTHER. IT HAS BEEN A YEAR OF MOURNING ONE body part after another, first the parts and then my mother. Losing the teeth was a blow but there are replacements that only you and your immediate family know about and, while chewing is never the same again, you can pass through public places undetected. You realize there will come a day in the distant future when there will be an emergency of sorts and you'll be asked to remove the dentures in case you gag on a piece of medical apparatus and people other than immediate family will frequent your bedside while you lie there toothless. But you can bring in a nurse with a hypodermic full of morphine to inject you until you forget the gap in your gums. Or you can imagine yourself so old and wise and full of the grace of God that you glow, literally glow, with an inner light while the assorted people at the bedside soak it up like the sun, eyes closed.

I never felt terribly connected to my ovaries, never fully understood the egg business and how it all fits together but I had a fleeting, mournful flash of two branch-like affairs lying spent in a kidney basin. I felt something like grief but only because they lay there so anonymously and unsung. I also wondered (and still do) about the Second Coming of Christ and if, when the dead are raised and we are given our incorruptible bodies, will they be exchanged part for part? And if so, will my assorted teeth and shrivelled ovaries rise from unexpected places, maybe the shoreline of Japan, while the rest of me lifts off from Vancouver Island?

The uterus was the wrenching one. If someone had told me before the surgery that I had a deep, psychic tie to it, I wouldn't have believed them. As it was, I lay there afterwards feeling as though I'd been gutted like a fish. I have vague recollections of my gynecologist coming in between injections, smelling fresh of the outdoors and younger women. I especially remember looking at his thin gold watch on the wrist of the hand that severed my uterus. He told me it looked like a purse embroidered with varicose veins. Perhaps it was the morphine . . . I had crazy dreams all that week running in stop-gap motion:

I am in an exclusive store looking at evening bags, a display of them, some with pearls, some with sequins, very small and elegant. The gynecologist enters the room with a young woman on his arm. She's all hair and legs. They approach the display table and he studies the evening bags, his manicured hand passing like a benediction over each one. The young woman flings back her head and laughs in a low, throaty manner exposing a mouthful of perfect white teeth, more than she needs. The gynecologist picks a black satin bag studded with diamonds and dangles it tauntingly in front of the young woman. She wets her lips seductively with her tongue, opens her mouth and takes little bites at the bag. They walk away laughing. I go back to the display table and there in the middle of the other bags is my little uterus with a handle and a clasp looking quite jaunty despite the varicose veins.

The third day after surgery was the worst. They removed the catheter and I found I had no control over my bladder. I kept peeing the bed. The nurses turned nasty. The gynecologist sailed in wearing his O.R. mask like a pendant around his neck, his greens unbuttoned on his chest, the nurses fluttering behind him.

"We're going to have to re-catheterize, you know, if you continue," he tells me with all the authority of his assorted degrees and the nurses behind him.

My husband and four daughters visit that night. They stand and stare at me. My youngest asks if I'm going to die. They watch my television and eat my supper. They wrap my pudding in paper towels to take home and eat later. I try to tell my husband how I feel. "Gutted," I explain, "like a fish."

He is playing with the levers at the foot of my bed. "This one raises her head and this one her feet." My daughters take turns at the controls. "And with this one," he demonstrates, "you can raise the whole middle section of the bed."

I hide my vulnerability, push it down into my strangely empty abdomen. I have recurring dreams of spawning salmon. Some nights I'm looking down on the river from a bridge and other nights I am in the water:

The gynecologist is standing on the riverbank casting his rod. I can see his gold watch quite clearly, the manicured hand winding the reel purposefully, a hint of sensuality in the black mat of hair between the watch and cuff. He is wearing a plaid hunting jacket like the other fishermen but you can feel the summa cum laude *in his bearing. My belly is swollen with eggs and bruised from the rocks. Male salmon infiltrate the ranks, like fools popping randomly out of the water. One of them has a black beard like my husband. The husband fish begins to tire. His eyes are unfocused and bulging. He has an orgasm in the water. I can see it spreading like a cloud beneath his tail. I feel a surge of rage. He has lost interest in the fertilizing. I head off to the spawning ground without him. Other salmon swim frantically beside me. I can feel their bloated femininity pushing in from all sides. It is uphill all the way. We are moving so slowly, the seagulls assume we are dead and remove the eyes from some of us. The gynecologist follows, climbing with agility, casting often.*

I'm standing on the bridge, looking down at the spawning ground. The gynecologist is there with a young nurse. She is holding an electric razor in one hand and an evening bag made out of my uterus in the other. The gynecologist is manipulating one of her breasts. She opens her mouth and purrs. It sounds like an electric razor. Her teeth are perfect and well aligned, too numerous to count.

I am in the water again. All around me the females are resigning. They allow their bodies to float to the surface. The gynecologist is angry that no one is biting the lure. He throws his reel on the ground and begins to pull us out by our tails and pass us to the nurse. She places us side by side on the rocks, dips a brush in a pot of barbecue sauce, bastes our bellies, and begins to shave us.

There is a dead salmon on the operating table. The medical staff are covered in scales and everything smells of fish. The gynecologist enters the operating theatre wearing a tuxedo. He's carrying a conductor's baton. He taps it three times on the salmon's belly and raises his hands. Vivaldi's "Suite for Four Seasons" flows out over the sound system. I wake up in the recovery room and a young nurse is adjusting my IV. I tell her I feel gutted. She smiles broadly and plunges a hypodermic in my side. I watch detached while the gynecologist and the nurse have intercourse at the foot of my bed.

My husband and daughters have adapted well in my absence and look openly hostile to receiving an invalid. The sheets are clean on my bed and there's a supply of soft food in the refrigerator, but the territories have been redefined while I was away. My daughters have taken over my former spaces, the few that I had, and the house feels too full of undiluted estrogen, most of it theirs. For the first time I resent their teenaged bodies and I'm glad my bedroom is upstairs away from the hub of them, even though I have to yell for my pudding. They carry on as though I'm not here, the daughters of my discarded uterus, downstairs.

My father calls to see how I am. His voice is flat. Mother is groaning in the background. The sound permeates the atmosphere like a foghorn, dull but persistent. I tell him I feel gutted like a fish. He says Mother has been sick in the night. I ask him if he's called the doctor. He has. The doctor thinks she's failing.

"Why can't I go to the party?" my daughter whines from the foot of the bed. She is wearing a tight skirt and her nose has been pierced. Her breasts have grown since I saw her last. All their breasts have grown, filling up spaces I can ill afford. Four ripe bosoms, fruit of a forgotten womb. Smelling blood and a common cause, they all join her at the bedside. My body shrivels under the covers, my phantom uterus shudders. I can hear the hockey game on the television downstairs. I can see my husband watching, eyes unfocused, oblivious to the ensuing bloodbath upstairs. They take turns calling me a witch. No other mother on the face of the earth is like me, they say. Every other mother lets their daughters go to parties. I close my eyes and lie there impassively. That night I dream of medical waste:

On the concrete floor of a hospital basement there is a large vat filled with bits of bone, blood-soaked sponges, and my uterus. A young woman pulls the vat on a wheeled trolley down a hall into a small, airless room. She opens a manhole on the floor and tilts the vat on its side. The contents slide out. I can hear the roar of the sewer down below. I race out of the hospital and run down the road above the sewer towards the outfall by the sea. My daughters drive by with their boyfriends. They are dressed seductively and there is loud music coming from the car. I reach Ogden Point out of breath and my daughters are on the beach with their boyfriends. As the medical waste reaches the outfall and silently discharges the bits of bone, blood-soaked sponges, and my uterus into the sea, I creep behind a large piece of driftwood and watch. My daughters' boyfriends have turned into four perfect replicas of my gynecologist, each one wearing a gold watch. Their movements are smooth and perfected as their manicured hands begin to slowly undress my daughters.

My uterus rides on an incoming wave. It looks poised and very confident, like a seasoned surfer. It deposits itself at their feet. A bag lady walks by groaning like a foghorn. She looks out of place at this time of night. She stops in front of my daughters and their gynecologists. She is very, very old, maybe a witch. My uterus is just sitting there. She chants some kind of incantation. I only catch every other word. She turns to the west and does something with feathers and smoke. The girls look impressed, perhaps a bit frightened. The gynecologists have stopped undressing them. She repeats the procedure to the north, to the east and the south. I'm not sure why but I like her. She picks up my uterus and holds it out before them. It is glowing from an inner source of light. Two prominent varicose veins regroup on its surface, surge with blood, and form lips. It smiles provocatively. It has many, many white teeth, several rows of them, sharp and hooked underneath like those of a shark. The bag lady-witch woman pulls two badly elongated breasts out of her vest and gets them moving in circles, counter-clockwise. She twirls them with increasing fury above the gynecologists' heads. The gynecologists watch transfixed. Their eyes are bulging and unfocused. My uterus, sensing a vulnerable moment, rushes at their crotches, teeth bared. Not one of them, not one, is spared.

Six weeks after surgery the gynecologist informs me I am on the road to recovery. Later that day, my mother's doctor tells us she has two, maybe three days to live.

My sister and I keep the bedside vigil. Mother is peaceful, ready to resign. We watch her slowly releasing her body to death. After it is over we send Father out of the room. He is spent. We prepare her little body, the receptacle of our lives, for the grave. We cleanse the hidden parts of her she no longer feels or needs.

We have Vivaldi's "Suite for Four Seasons" playing at the funeral. My sister and I sit in the front row, the coffin before us. Behind us are our daughters.

Kathryn LeCorre